CAPE MAY RAINDROPS

CLAUDIA VANCE

CHAPTER ONE

Dolly stood on her tippy toes on the Seahorse Inn's porch as she tried to hang a decorative plastic Easter egg on one of the hanging plant hooks. "There we go," she said as she stood back and wiped her hands on her apron.

Kim squinted her eyes to see from the other side of the porch where she had just finished propping the new yellow pillows on the white rocking chairs. "Oh, that looks nice, Dolly, but I thought we were hanging them from that cherry blossom tree over there," she said, pointing.

Dolly looked over at the fluffy pink flowering tree and then back at Kim. "Oh, we've got plenty more to hang on the tree too."

Kim smiled, then darted inside after hearing the telephone ring in the foyer. "I'll get it."

Dolly bent down to grasp the woven basket full of ornamental Easter eggs and carried it down the porch steps towards the tree, nearly tripping over Margaret, who was on her hands and knees near the bushes.

"Oh, I'm sorry. Didn't see you, Margaret," Dolly said with a slight chuckle.

Margaret smiled as she showed off her floral gardening gloves that were now stained brown. "I figured I'd lay down some mulch around these spring bulbs. Look how much nicer it looks," she said while standing up and taking a few steps back to see it at a better angle.

Dolly nodded. "It's beautiful. It looks so tidy and cleaned up now, and those yellow daffodils and bright-red tulips against the blue siding on the inn are gorgeous. Just makes it pop."

"That's what I was going for," Margaret said as she nudged Dolly playfully with her shoulder.

"OK, I'm back. Just had to take a call from one of our couples coming Easter weekend," Kim said as she walked down the porch stairs to meet Dolly and Margaret.

Suddenly, a noise sounded from around the side of the inn, and then Liz appeared, struggling with two rakes and some hedge clippers as she walked closer. She tossed everything on the green grass, then took a deep breath. "Well, it's officially spring. Guess it's time to clean up the ol' girl after that treacherous winter."

Margaret bent down to smell some pink hyacinths that had started to bloom near the birdbath. "Oh, it wasn't that bad of a winter. I mean, I've seen worse."

Liz rolled her eyes. "Not that bad? It felt like it was below freezing the whole month of February, and that snowstorm we got? The kids were off school for *three* whole days. *Three*! Those makeup days are going to cut into our summer plans when school is extended in June."

Dolly and Kim nodded in agreement as they hung the pastel-colored Easter eggs with twine from the tree.

Margaret shrugged. "Well, maybe you're right, but the girls loved their snow days. We found that great little hill on our property for sledding, and we must have spent hours out there that one day. Remember?"

Liz chuckled. "How could I forget? I couldn't get the boys

to leave. Greg had to bribe them with a round of board games, but then that turned into an all-night event that we weren't expecting back at the house."

Margaret watched as some robins flew onto the lawn near them and started searching through the grass for worms, then bit her lip as she looked up at the gray clouds that were starting to overtake the bright-blue sky. "Looks like we may be getting some rain. We probably should hurry with this out here."

Liz nodded as she picked up the hedge clippers and started deadheading the hydrangeas. "So, we're still planning an Easter brunch for our guests that weekend, right?"

Margaret nodded. "Yes, well, we have to now. It was part of our Easter weekend package deal, and don't forget the community Easter egg hunt across the street on the beach that we're putting together."

Liz snipped a dried-up brown hydrangea bloom bunch and studied it. "That's right. I forgot how much organizing and planning we have to do, and it's only what? Eleven days away?"

Irene poked her head out of the front door and a lovely baked-bread smell wafted into the air towards everyone's noses. "How are y'all doing out there?" she said, glancing up at the now ominous-looking sky.

Margaret placed some cement gnomes with green moss hats near the bottom of the steps as everyone else worked quickly to finish what they were doing. "Oh, we're doing good. Mostly finished for now, I think," she said as she glanced up at Irene.

Jackie stuck her head out the door next to Irene and looked up at the sky along with her. "It's going to pour any minute. I can feel it. My bones never lie."

Dolly and Kim chuckled as they each tied some of the last Easter eggs to a tree branch. "Our old achy bones don't lie either," Kim said.

Just then a crack of thunder could be heard in the distance, causing the women to hop back, startled. Liz quickly picked up the rakes with the clippers and walked them to the back shed while Margaret found a spot under the cherry blossom tree out of the rain.

"Get inside before you get soaked," Irene yelled from the front door as Dolly and Kim ran up the steps to the safety of the porch.

Liz came running from the backyard with her jacket held over her head, then she walked up the steps and stood on the front porch, glancing down at Margaret who was fixing a couple Easter eggs that had popped open on the tree. "What are you doing? Get up here."

Margaret smiled. "It's fine. It's barely raining right now. Plus, Dave is coming to get me any minute." Liz sighed and shrugged as she headed inside the warm and delicious-smelling B&B with Dolly and Kim. It was quiet outside with just Margaret there now, aside from a passing car here and there on Beach Avenue.

She fixed the last Easter egg, then paused and took a deep breath as she looked up at the beautiful pink flowers above her on the tree. A few petals fell onto her hair and face, when suddenly another clap of thunder rang out and the skies opened up.

Sheets of rain fell just as Dave's truck pulled into the driveway. He rolled down his window and shielded the rain as he laughed while looking at his wife hunkered down under a tree. "Whatcha doing, hon?"

Margaret peered at him through the rainfall as large puddles formed all around the lawn. "Me? Oh, you know, a little this and that," she yelled jokingly through the pounding rain.

Abby and Harper climbed up to the front seat and leaned over Dave to stick their heads out the window. "Mom? What are you doing?"

Margaret shook her head with a chuckle as she leapt out

from under the tree, raced towards the passenger side door, swung it open, hopped into the seat, and slammed it shut as though her life depended on it. She sat there, drenched, trying to catch her breath while Dave playfully tussled her hair. "So, where to, birthday girl?

Margaret shook her head and laughed. "Birthday girl? It's not until April 4."

Dave shrugged as the rain beat down noisily on the truck while they idled in the driveway. "So? It's March 29 now … that means it's six days away. We're celebrating your birth *week*."

Harper and Abby peered over the front seats. "Oh yay! Does that mean we're doing something fun every day this week?' Abby asked with excitement in her eyes.

Dave nodded as he shifted the gear into reverse. "I was thinking something along those lines. I've got a few things up my sleeve."

"Alright!" Harper yelled out as she leaned back into the seat and buckled her seat belt along with Abby.

Dave kept his foot on the brake as he reached over and touched Margaret's hand that rested on her leg. "I was thinking we could start the celebration tonight. Instead of cooking, I figured we could head down Beach Avenue to Taco Caballito Tequileria?"

Margaret widely grinned. "I think I could definitely go for tacos. What do you think, girls?"

Abby pointed towards the street. "Wow! You must be mind readers. I was just thinking about tacos."

"Me too," Harper said as she rubbed her stomach.

Margaret laughed as Dave reversed the truck out of the driveway while the rain continued to pour down.

* * *

Meanwhile across town, Judy stood in their finished basement with her hand on her hip, looking around the cluttered space. "What *is* all of this?"

Bob opened the door from the laundry area and stepped out holding four folding chairs and leaned them against the wall. "What is *what*?" he asked while looking around the room.

Judy sighed. "*That*," she said pointing to a big stack of storage bins in the corner.

Bob chuckled. "That's everything we brought over from the old house years ago and never unpacked. Who knows what's in there."

Judy rolled her eyes. "We've really got to have a yard sale to get rid of all of this stuff."

Bob nodded in agreement, then walked up the stairs towards the back door. "I'm going in the garage to get the folding tables. How many did you say you wanted?"

Judy counted on her fingers. "Well, Linda and her family, Debbie and her family, Carol, Jack, the kids, our daughters and their husbands, and the grandkids ... and well, jeez. I'd better go write this down," Judy said as she walked up the stairs behind Bob.

Bob shook his head and laughed. "Well, I guess I'll grab all the tables and bring them in. I think the rain just started to die down a little. Might be good to grab them now. We'll figure out logistics as Easter gets closer. Sound like a plan?"

Judy walked over to the kitchen table and sat down with her notebook and pen to begin writing. "Sounds good, dear. I think having Easter here with my siblings and their families along with our family is going to be wonderful. I'm really excited for this."

Bob gazed around their small house as uncertainty set in. "You think everyone's going to fit? I mean, the last time we did something like this was at the old house, which was much bigger than this rancher here."

Judy scratched her head in thought as she looked towards

the living room. "Well, I think we'll figure it out. I'm over the moon at the prospect of having everyone over … just like old times. It feels like for the last fifteen years we've spent every Easter in Pennsylvania at Linda and Mike's. I think we're due for a change up."

Just then, Judy's cell phone rang, and Bob took that as his cue to finally go out to the garage and bring in the folding tables.

"Linda!" Judy said happily. She stood up from the table and made her way to the couch where she flopped down and propped her arm on two throw pillows.

"Hey there, Judy. Thought I'd check in and see how things are over there in Jersey," she said as she talked with the phone on speaker as she sewed a patch onto the quilt she was making.

Judy smiled. "Well, things are good. We're starting to get ready for Easter dinner. I can't believe it's coming up so soon. I'm excited for us all to be together again."

Linda finished sewing, then stopped the machine. "Yeah, about that …"

Judy shifted her eyes. "Yeah?"

Linda sighed as she held her quilt block up to examine it. "Well … Carol and I had a little falling out."

Judy sat up straight. "What do you mean?"

Linda sighed. "Her and I made plans to have lunch the other day over at Miller's Deli. I forgot, as I was at a quilting meetup and had my phone turned off, and she ended up going and eating alone. Well, by the time I got out of my meetup and turned on my phone, I had a bajillion text messages from her. They started out with *Hi, I'm here. Where are you?* and then the last ones were so full of anger and frustration that I don't want to repeat them. I guess she thought I was ignoring her. Well, I tried to call her and apologize, and she laid into me about 'the way I am' and how 'I've always been the inconsiderate sister.'"

Judy held her hand to her mouth. "I'm shocked. She didn't even give you a chance to explain yourself?"

Linda rolled her eyes. "Nope. She decided to unleash every single frustration she's ever had in her lifetime with me on the phone that day. I'm telling you, she brought something up about me taking her doll when we were in elementary school. Really, Carol? We're in our seventies. I mean c'mon! I ended up hanging up on her. I'm not taking that, nor should I."

Judy shook her head. "Well, you should really talk to her. We can't have all this animosity during Easter dinner."

Linda cut in. "Oh, I'm not coming if Carol is going to be there. I'm more upset about how she handled the situation than she is with me for forgetting about our lunch date. This has turned into a full-blown fight, I'm telling ya. We're not speaking. Well, I've got to go. This quilt top needs to be finished before I go grocery shopping. I'll give you a call tomorrow. Bye, Judy."

Bob walked in the back door carrying a long table just as Judy hung up the phone and made a loud groan. "Is everything alright?" Bob asked.

Judy took a deep breath. "Well, I just found out Linda and Carol aren't speaking over something stupid."

Bob set the table on the floor and scratched his head. "Really? That doesn't seem like them."

Judy sighed. "It doesn't, but then you didn't grow up in the same house as them. This is actually very reminiscent of our teenage years. Carol and Linda were constantly at each other's throats. Debbie would usually side with Linda, and well, I was always the neutral one trying to make everything better. I swear my parents probably wished they had all sons after dealing with us."

Bob laughed. "Looks like you may have to take on that peacemaker role again."

Judy walked next to Bob and flung her arms around him. "I don't want to deal with this childish drama. I'm too old for this. *We're* too old for this. I mean, this is so silly."

Bob, sensing that Judy was starting to get stressed, kissed

the top of her head. "Don't worry about it. They'll work it out. Plus, we probably don't have room for them anyway what with all these people coming. Let 'em stay home," he said with a chuckle.

Judy tried to hold in a laugh. "Hey, don't say that about my sisters," she said as she playfully nudged him.

CHAPTER TWO

Dale and Donna stood in their living room watching the noisy business of construction workers pulling out their old kitchen appliances in the Cape May Point home they now owned.

Dale smiled as he looked over at Donna. "This kitchen renovation is going to be a chef's dream."

Donna smiled back and took a long, deep sigh. "It really is. I'm thinking of all the wonderful meals we're going to make, and I can't wait to have friends and family over to enjoy it too."

Dale nodded as he watched two workers wheel their old refrigerator outside on a dolly. "Well, I guess we're eating out for the next couple of weeks. There goes the fridge."

Donna laughed. "Can't say I'm too upset about that. It'll be fun. All the restaurants are opened up again from winter break ... including yours and Greg's."

Dale looked at his watch. "That's right. Though, I think everyone feels a little rusty after that long winter hiatus. I've actually got to leave soon to get over there. You OK managing this?" he asked, motioning to the chaos and noise in the kitchen.

Donna flicked her hand. "Oh, I'm fine. I'll make sure to be

around for whatever questions they have. I've got my night class tonight, but they should be done well before that."

Dale reached to get his light canvas jacket from the coat rack, then picked up his keys off the table before leaning over to give Donna a kiss. "Perfect. I'll call you when I'm done, and maybe we can meet somewhere for dinner after your class."

Donna cocked her head to the side. "Well, I could just meet you at the restaurant?"

Dale thought for a moment. "I'm there all the time. I think tonight I'd like a little change. You know, go out and see how other restaurants are faring these days."

Donna reached up to give Dale a hug goodbye, and as she let go, her engagement ring snagged on his jacket, forcing her to lightly tug it off. She pulled her hand down and studied the antique diamond ring.

Dale watched her as she made sure the ring was still intact, then smiled. "We haven't really discussed wedding planning. We should probably get on that, no?"

Donna scratched her head. "Well, yeah … sure. Though, I'm not in a big rush. Are you? Why not enjoy this engagement for a bit. We'll start planning when it feels right, you know?"

Dale's heart sank a little. He was used to seeing other couples plan their weddings soon after becoming engaged. He'd proposed seven months ago, and they hadn't done much of anything since. Then again, they *had been* busy. They'd bought the home they'd been renting in the late fall, and started renovations almost immediately, on top of Donna's full-time college classes and Dale's new restaurant.

Donna snapped her fingers in front of Dale's glazed over eyes. "Dale. You in there?"

Dale immediately snapped to. "Oh, sorry. Went into deep thought there," he said as he glanced at the clock by the TV. "Wow, I'm running late. I'd better go. I'll give you call later," he said as he kissed Donna on the forehead and headed out the door.

Ten minutes later, Dale parked a block away from Donna's Restaurant, hopped out of his car, and started walking. As he got closer, he could see a lot of people waiting outside. For a Thursday lunch, that was unusual unless it was summer.

Dale walked inside to find his hostess, Jean, frantically walking around putting silverware and placemats on tables with one hand while taking a reservation on the phone in the other. "Jean, you OK?"

Jean stopped for a moment and held her finger up to signal that she needed a minute. "OK, thank you, Mr. Deacon. We'll see you this evening for your reservation at five o'clock with your party of five. I'll put it on the books," she said as she hung the phone up and stuck it in her pocket and looked over at Dale while shaking her head. "Frank, our manager, has been stuck in traffic on the parkway for an hour now, and we had two servers call out due to being sick, and two cooks were no-shows."

Dale's eyes widened. "You're kidding. Who didn't show? Not the two cooks I just interviewed and hired the other day?"

Jean rolled her eyes. "Yes, them. What a great way to start a new job," she said sarcastically.

Dale shook his head and sighed. "This happened at the beginning of the month, too, when we reopened. Why do people interview for jobs they don't want to show up to?"

Jean shrugged. "Beats me. I mean, I showed up."

Dale patted Jean on the back. "You always do. Thank you, Jean," he said as he glanced back at all the people waiting outside. "So, all those people waiting … is it because we're down two servers, I'm assuming?"

Jean nodded. "Yes. Since lunch is never that busy in the off-season, we usually have three servers on, and Marcy is the only one here. She normally only has three or four tables at a time, but she's running all ten tables, and I'm trying to help out as best I can."

Dale sighed. "OK, well, call April and Layla. I know they

were looking to pick up shifts today. See if they'll come in. In the meantime, I'm going to check on the kitchen, and see if we need extra help there. If they're good, I'll help Marcy out and take some tables."

Suddenly a loud crash resounded next to them and water splashed all over Dale as their new college-aged busser, Ernie—who was still learning the ropes—dropped his bin of dirty dishes and glasses.

"Oh, no. I'm so sorry. I don't know what happened," Ernie said as he quickly started picking everything up and putting it back into the bin.

Dale kneeled down to help him. "It's OK. You'll get the hang of this soon enough, I'm sure."

Jean stared down at the mess all over the floor, then back at the host stand with a line forming in front of it. "I'd love to help, guys, but I've got to get back to my hosting duties."

Dale stood up and brushed the water off his pants. "Seat me four tables, and I'll be right out after I check on the kitchen."

Jean shifted her eyes. "Four tables at once? Are you sure, Dale?"

Dale shrugged. "How hard can it be?"

Jean chuckled. "Alright then. I'm seating them. Let me know if you need help."

* * *

Two hours later, the lunch rush had finally died down, and Dale was ready to collapse from nonstop running around. He'd hardly been able to keep up with refilling drinks, taking orders, and running food and beverages to both his and Marcy's tables.

Dale took a breather and leaned on the host stand. "Jean, as the owner, I'm always pleased when we're busy, but right now, I couldn't be happier that we aren't. I forgot how much work serving is," he said right as his dinner-shift employees started walking through the door.

Jean put on her jacket to go home. "Well, it was a team effort, and we got it done. Thankfully, Carlos was able to come in and help in the kitchen. Frank eventually got here too. I never did hear back from April or Layla about coming in. They probably made other plans since they weren't on the schedule."

Marcy walked up to them with her apron in her hands. "I think that was the most chaotic shift I've ever worked. Then again, I made more tips than I do on a busy summer shift. We should have people call out more often," she said half-jokingly.

Dale chuckled. "No, we shouldn't."

Marcy walked out the door, and Dale reached into his apron and pulled out two twenties. "Jean, for your efforts today. I'm the owner, and it doesn't feel right keeping this," he said as he gave another forty dollars to Ernie, who was standing nearby.

"Thank you, Dale. It's appreciated. I'm heading home to see my husband and kids now and tell them about this crazy day," Jean said, then she disappeared out the door.

Dale pulled his phone out of his pocket and smiled as he called Donna about dinner plans. He sure was glad they decided on going somewhere other than his restaurant this evening.

* * *

Over at West End Garage, Sarah was browsing the many different spring-inspired items for sale at sellers' booths with Sam.

Sam picked up a blue truck and held it up for Sarah to see. "Look! They sell toys here."

Sarah chuckled. "That's an antique collectable truck. I'd put that down."

Sam shrugged and set the truck down, then glanced over at Sarah as he picked up an old Easter book. "How long are we going to be here?"

Sarah looked at the time on her cell phone. "Well, your dad said to meet him at the dock at five, so maybe another twenty minutes?"

Sam sighed as he flipped through the pages of the book, then set it carefully down before turning around and noticing someone familiar shopping. "Mom!" Sam yelled out as he approached the woman.

Sarah looked over to see Chris's ex-wife, Roberta, hugging Sam.

"Hi, Roberta. Funny seeing you here," Sarah said with a warm smile.

Roberta flung her perfectly styled blonde hair behind her shoulder as Sam walked off to look at a whole section of different hats. "Sarah ... I haven't seen you in a while."

Sarah shrugged. "Yeah, it's been what? Some months? Chris always seems to be dropping Sam off at your house when I'm working or out."

Roberta took a deep breath. "Well, what are you two up to?"

Sarah looked at her cell phone. "We're killing time before we're meeting Chris at the dock. I figured we'd stop in here. There's always neat things to browse."

Roberta picked up a vintage green pitcher and studied it. "Oh? What are you all doing at the dock?"

Sarah glanced at a hand-painted teacup with cheerful spring flowers, just the thing she'd been looking to add to the Book Nook's supply. "He's taking us on our own personal sunset cruise. Then, probably dinner."

Roberta tried not to show any emotion on her face. "That sounds ... nice."

Sarah used her left hand to push her brown hair out of her eyes, unknowingly flashing her gorgeous diamond ring.

Roberta's eyes widened. "Is that ... an engagement ring?"

Sam walked up with a bucket hat on just in time to hear the question. "Yes, Dad and Sarah are engaged, Mom. Where've you been?"

Roberta felt her heart race. "I ... I didn't know this."

Sam rolled his eyes. "I told you. Remember?"

Roberta looked down at Sam with confusion. "When?"

Sam shrugged. "I don't know. Last year when it happened."

Roberta looked back at Sarah. "I'm sorry. I must have not heard him. Anyway ... congratulations," she said with a forced smile.

"Well, thank you," Sarah said.

"I guess I'm just surprised."

Sarah paused for a moment in shock. "Surprised about what?"

Roberta shifted her eyes to make sure Sam wasn't listening. "That he proposed."

"Why?" Sarah asked baffled.

"Well, you know he blames marriage for ruining us. He told me when we divorced that he never wanted to get married again. It wasn't for him. I guess he's had a change of mind," Roberta said while glancing around the room.

Sarah shrugged. "Oh, I know. He told me all of that."

Roberta looked at Sam. "Dear, why don't you go look at those toys down there."

Sam sighed. "Why? I already looked at them."

Roberta clenched her teeth. "Please just do it."

"Fine," Sam said as he walked twenty feet away.

Roberta glanced back at Sarah. "I would just be careful with him. That's all I'm going to say."

Sarah looked back at Sam, then at Roberta in confusion. "With Sam? I'm always careful with him. He's in good hands with me. Don't worry."

Roberta shook her head. "No, with Chris."

Sarah was taken aback. "What?"

Roberta took a deep breath. "I suspect he was cheating on me all that time. He always seemed to be working extra late on the boat and taking phone calls outside. He blames marriage as a general concept for our demise, but I don't believe it for a second. Something else was going on there."

Sarah paused, not sure how to even respond to Roberta. She reached over to touch some brass candlestick holders to try and avoid the discussion they were getting into.

Roberta grabbed Sarah's left hand and stared hard at the engagement ring. "It's a nice ring. Did you pick it out?"

Sarah pulled her hand away abruptly. "I didn't. Chris surprised me with it. You know, we've really got to go."

Roberta pursed her lips. "How did he propose?"

Sarah looked around for Sam. "Sam, are you ready?"

Sam glanced up happily from the toys he was looking at. "Yes. I've *been* ready," he said as he marched over.

Roberta kept staring at Sarah, waiting for an answer.

"The beach. Our friends were there with us," Sarah said with an awkward smile as she glanced at the flashy ring on her finger.

Suddenly, all the noise surrounding them in the room became quiet as she remembered something. The evening of the engagement, Chris seemed to have swapped rings with Dale right before he proposed to her on the beach. How could she have forgotten? She never did get the full answer to that.

"Earth to Sarah," Roberta said as she waved her hands in front of Sarah.

Sarah rubbed her hands over her face before pulling her phone out of her pocket and looking at the time. "It was nice seeing you, Roberta. We've really got to be heading out. Chris will bring Sam over after dinner, I'm sure."

Sam sighed. "Can't I just sleep over at Dad's?"

Roberta shook her head. "You've got school tomorrow."

"Well, bye, Mom," Sam said as he hugged her, then started

towards the door, leaving Sarah and Roberta standing there alone.

"I'd better go," Sarah said as she walked fast to catch up with Sam.

Roberta stood there shaking her head just as another customer backed up into her, causing her to stumble back.

Sarah and Sam made it outside into the misty air, and Sarah couldn't have been happier to get away from Roberta. They hopped into Sarah's car, and as they buckled up, and Sarah put her hand on the steering wheel, she stared at her ring for a moment in thought. One thing she knew was certain: Before they got married, they needed to lay everything out in the open. She needed to know what happened with the rings that night they got engaged, and now the truth about why Roberta and Chris's marriage didn't work out.

CHAPTER THREE

Judy and Bob sat on the Cape May-Lewes Ferry as it started the hour-long journey towards Lewes, Delaware at 7 a.m. They had found some nice seating on the upper deck with perfect views of the water.

Bob put his arm around Judy as the breeze picked up. "Glad we decided on bringing the car this time."

Judy chuckled. "Oh, you don't want to ride our bikes again?"

Bob shook his head and laughed. "That was a nightmare."

Judy nodded. "We pedaled off the boat and found it was a fifteen-mile bike ride—not two!—to where I wanted to go."

Bob cut in. "Then, my bike chain got loose …."

Judy laughed. "And my tire went flat …."

Bob shook his head. "So, we found some random bike rack and then walked what felt like miles to find something, anything to eat."

"We were starving. That's for sure," Judy said as the wind picked up, blowing her hair around.

"That was quite a day," Bob said, chuckling and shaking his head.

Judy turned to face Bob. "Now that I think of it, every time we've taken the ferry, it's turned out to be an adventure."

Bob furrowed his brow. "Oh yeah? What am I missing?"

Judy watched as two people walked by with drinks, then turned her gaze to the indoor bar. Let's go over there and get a drink while I remember …"

Bob glanced inside at the bar area. "Judy, it's seven in the morning."

Judy waved her hand in the air. "I'm talking iced tea, orange juice, or coffee, silly."

They both stood up and walked inside the ferry, where Bob ordered drinks from the bartender.

Judy turned to Bob. "OK, I remember now. Before that bike fiasco, back when the girls were in elementary school, we took the ferry to Rehoboth Beach."

The bartender set down two orange juices on paper napkins in front of them, and Bob took a long sip before bringing the drinks to a nearby table where they both took seats.

"Oh yes, how could I forget. We spent a weekend there—a great one, at that. What went wrong?" Bob asked.

Judy laughed. "You don't remember? On the boardwalk, or near it, was that huge arcade with those claw machines. You know, where you put a quarter in and try to grab a stuffed animal with the claw that drops down?"

Bob nodded. "That's right. There were stuffed dinosaurs in that one machine that I figured out how to win almost every time."

Judy took a sip of her orange juice. "You became obsessed with winning them. Our entire weekend revolved around being at this arcade. We had trash bags full of plush dinosaurs. Then, when you'd won enough, you traded them in for those gigantic stuffed dinosaurs. The girls were having the time of their lives. Even they were winning them."

Bob sighed happily. "Ah, the good ol' days. We had a time, didn't we?"

Judy smiled and shook her head. "Well, it was fun and all until it was time to go home. We had that little two-door sedan at the time that the four of us barely fit in."

Bob's eyes widened. "Now I see where you're going with this. We had no space to fit all those stuffed animals—both human-sized and small—into that tiny car."

Judy laughed until tears streamed down her face. "None of the large dinosaurs fit, and we only got one trash bag of the smaller ones in the trunk. We had to give away the rest. We marched right back into the arcade with the rest of those stuffed animals and handed them out to all the kids in there."

Bob nodded. "It may have been more fun giving them away than actually winning them."

Judy looked out towards the water as the sun's rays began to hit the upper deck. "Finally, a gorgeous day after all the rain we've been getting. It's the perfect day to take the ferry."

Bob looked at the weather forecast on his phone. "Enjoy it while you can. We've got lots of rain coming up, including later today, by the way. Any news with Linda and Carol? Have they made amends?"

Judy shrugged. "I don't know. I sure hope so. They all said they are coming for Easter, though, and I'm holding them to it. As far as the drama, I've decided I'm going to stay out of it."

Bob took another sip of his juice, then stood up and rubbed his arms. "Sounds smart. Oh yeah, I forgot to tell you that Audrey left a message that they are coming for Easter too …. Are we going to be able to fit everyone at the house?"

Judy nodded confidently. "Sure. The more the merrier. We'll figure it out. Plus, I'm sure we can put tables and chairs outside as well. I've got some ideas up my sleeve, don't you worry."

Bob motioned towards the windows. "Wanna head back

outside? Maybe enjoy this nice weather a little more before the rain comes?"

Judy stood up and smiled, then put her arm through his. "You read my mind. Lead the way, dear."

* * *

Liz walked in from a long day dealing with interior design clients, threw her keys into the basket by the door, and let out a loud groan as she put down her heavy laptop bag and took off her rain-soaked jacket. She noticed a TV playing in the background.

"Hello?" Liz said out loud, confused as to who would be home at three thirty.

Nobody answered, but then loud giggles came from the living room.

Liz walked through the kitchen and spotted her twin sons, Michael and Steven, each sitting on a couch with a girl beside them.

Liz's eyes widened. "Why aren't you two at baseball practice?"

Michael motioned to the sliding glass door. "It's raining, like, hard. They canceled."

Steven nodded. "So we walked home."

Liz paused for a moment. "You walked home in the rain? That's a long walk, and who are your … friends?" Liz asked looking at the two girls, who seemed to be sitting very close to her sons.

Michael started speaking, when one of the girls chimed in. "I'm Hailey, and that's Jamie. We're in the same grade."

Liz nodded. "Oh, OK. So, you all know each other from school?"

Jamie giggled as she nudged Steven. "Yes, but we also have softball practice on the fields next to where the boys practice. We live even further than Michael and Steven, so they invited us to come in while we wait for our parents to get home from work and come pick us up."

Liz smiled. "Well, that was nice of you, Michael and Steven. Would you like some snacks while you wait?" Liz asked as she walked into the kitchen and looked into the fridge.

Steven shook his head. "We already made a cheese plate with a salami rose, olives, grapes, and nuts. Whipped it together real quick. Michael and I copied what Dad does. Come have some, Mom."

Liz shut the fridge door with a smile on her face, then walked into the living room to see the gorgeous charcuterie board. Her sons were already learning how to host people and they didn't even know it. She popped a couple of kalamata olives into her mouth and plucked out a few pieces of cheese.

Moments later, Greg walked in the house. "Hey, everyone. Just stopping in to grab a few things before I head back to the restaurant— Oh, hi there," Greg said noticing the two girls. The boys had never invited girls over before or even talked about girls. Their lives seemed to revolve around sports and video games.

Liz smirked. "That's Hailey and Jamie. They walked home together and are waiting for their parents to pick them up."

Greg shrugged as he walked around the kitchen opening drawers looking for his cell phone charger. "Well, that's cool. Feel free to snack from the fridge—"

Liz cut him off. "Oh, your sons already made one of your famous charcuterie boards."

Greg stopped what he was doing. "You're kidding. I've never seen them make food in my life except peanut butter and jelly sandwiches."

Liz smiled and reached into the cabinet above the stove. "Well, they've been learning by watching you, that's for sure. Is this what you're looking for?" she asked as she pulled out a long dangling USB cable.

"Yes!" Greg said enthusiastically as he took it from Liz,

then kissed her on the cheek. "I've got to hurry out of here for our pre-dinner employee meeting at Heirloom. We're going over our first Easter brunch at the restaurant. Usually, we offer Easter dinner, but this year, I'm thinking brunch."

Liz nodded. "Sounds like a plan, and now you can make it to my mom's big Easter dinner this year."

A car horn beeped outside, and Hailey and Jamie popped up from the couch.

"Your ride seems to be here, girls. It was nice meeting you," Liz said as she walked towards the front door to open it.

Steven and Michael followed behind the girls and stopped at the open door with them before saying their goodbyes and closing the door.

Liz glanced at Greg. "I really like Hailey and Jamie. They seem nice."

Greg chuckled.

Liz looked at Greg, confused. "What's so funny?"

Greg hugged Liz, then picked up his car keys in the basket by the door. "Nothing, dear. I've got to go before I'm late. Call me if you need anything."

* * *

Margaret lounged on a chair with a glass of wine at the beach house she and Dave owned, and glanced at her husband as he set the table, preparing to serve his home-cooked meal.

"What smells so good?" she asked as she stood up.

Dave took a deep breath before walking into the kitchen to open the oven. "I made us lasagna and garlic bread. I figure afterwards we can go walk along the beach and watch the sunset over the bay."

"This is wonderful, Dave, but you're doing too much. I don't need a whole 'birthday week' of festivities," Margaret said while shaking her head in disbelief.

Dave stood up from the oven, holding the hot lasagna dish

with two potholders, and brought it into the dining room to place it on the trivet. "It's nothing. I enjoy spoiling you. You ready to eat? Maybe we can start on the salad while the lasagna sits for a bit."

"Salad too?" Margaret asked shocked.

Dave pulled a big clear bowl of lettuce, tomatoes, carrots, and cucumbers out of the fridge in one hand, and a jar of his homemade balsamic dressing in the other. "Yep. Let's eat."

Margaret smiled and sat at the table as Dave placed the salad with tongs beside her, then lit two peach-colored taper candles in the middle of the table. "You even planned this perfectly—a romantic dinner while the girls are at their horse-back riding lesson."

Dave chuckled. "Thankfully, there's an indoor ring for them to ride in case it rains again."

Margaret dished some salad and dressing onto her plate and took a bite. "Oh, this is fresh and delicious, Dave. Well done."

Dave nodded as he took a bite of his. "Well, thank you. Wait till you taste the lasagna. It's my mom's recipe. It was always one of my favorites growing up."

"I can't wait," Margaret said with a smile, feeling completely happy.

By the time Margaret finished her salad, Dave was cutting and serving the lasagna, and just before she took her first bite, he slid an envelope across the table to her. "For you," Dave said as he flashed her a smile.

"What's this?" Margaret asked as she ate some of her lasagna.

"It's your birthday gift, but I have to give it to you now and not on your actual birthday," Dave said.

Margaret opened the envelope to see a piece of paper with a travel itinerary on it. "Florida? You got us tickets to Florida?" she asked, shocked.

Dave pointed to the paper. "Look at the date we leave."

Margaret scanned the paper until she came across the departure date, and then her eyes widened. "Tomorrow? Oh, Dave. I have to help get the Seahorse ready for our Easter weekend festivities and the girls—"

Dave cut in. "You'll be home by Monday, so it's a short trip, and I already arranged for the girls to stay with your parents, and I spoke to Liz. She has a plan for you two to start getting ready on Monday when you get home. We leave very early tomorrow to make the most of our two days there."

Margaret smiled. "What are we going to do?"

"We're going to visit my parents on their houseboat, lay on the beach, eat delicious food, drink delicious drinks. You know, relax and unwind," Dave said as he finished his last bite of his meal and walked into the kitchen.

Margaret bit her lip. "Well, that does sound nice," she said aloud as she pictured them in a hotel on a sunny beach.

Dave grabbed their dirty dishes, starting the cleanup process. "By the way, we're going to stay on a houseboat. I found one for rent that's docked right near my parents. I thought it would be a fun experience."

Margaret shrugged. "That sounds … interesting. I can't thank you enough for this gift," she said, bringing the rest of the dinner dishes into the kitchen.

Ten minutes later, after cleaning up, they put on some hoodies, and headed straight across the street to the bay as the sun was starting to set.

"I love this time of the year," Margaret said as she put her hand in Dave's as they walked along the beach. "The smell of the Easter lilies and hyacinths, the beauty of the red tulips and yellow daffodils. Cold winters just make you long for this and appreciate it even more when it comes."

Dave looked at Margaret with a smile on his face.

"What?" Margaret asked with a chuckle.

Dave sighed. "You just really know how to savor the little things that life has to offer. I admire that."

Margaret blushed then stopped and turned to look in the opposite direction down the beach. "I think the ferry should be arriving soon. Should we walk down and watch it come in?"

Dave nodded. "Great idea. Haven't done that in a while."

Sure enough, by the time they trekked down to the other side of the beach, the ferry was lit up and just pulling in. They watched as it slowly sailed on by, waving to passengers who didn't see them.

Margaret looked over at Dave and smiled as rain started to trickle from the sky. She held her arms up to feel each drop on the palms of her hands.

Dave looked ahead as the gray rain clouds covered the gorgeous orange-and-pink sunset. "Looks like we'd better head back now in case—"

Before he could say another word, the skies opened up, and the rain came pouring down as they ran down the beach back to the house, all the while laughing like kids.

CHAPTER FOUR

Late the next morning, Dave and Margaret landed in Daytona and drove their rental car to the marina where Dave's parents' boat was docked for the season and where their rental houseboat was located.

Dave parked their little blue sedan, stepped out and stretched his arms as he popped the trunk and pulled their suitcases out. "Whatcha doing in there?" he asked as he glanced at Margaret while she sat in the front seat looking at her phone.

Margaret put her sunglasses on, opened the car door, and stepped out, still looking at her phone. "Sorry, I was texting Liz. She's having a meeting at the Seahorse with the ladies about Easter weekend. I feel so guilty for not being there."

Dave shook his head. "Relax. Remember she said everything would be fine. I want you to enjoy this weekend. We're only here for two days after all."

Margaret sighed and reached for her suitcase handle, then rolled it behind Dave as they walked through the marina. "I guess you're right. It's only two days. I'll be back on Monday."

Dave nodded and put his arm around her shoulders and squeezed. "Everything will be fine. Now, I've got to locate someone to help us find which boat we're staying on."

Margaret pointed to a man walking around the dock checking on things. "There. Maybe he knows."

Dave walked out the doors to the dock, with Margaret behind him, and flagged the guy down with his arms. "Hey, there. Do you mind helping us for a minute? We're trying to figure out which boat we rented."

The guy bit his lip. "I don't know of anyone who has rentals in this marina."

Dave shifted his eyes, then pulled his phone out to look up his reservation. "Here's my confirmation. Two nights at Shoreline Marina. This is a photo of the boat."

The man shook his head. "I've never seen that boat in my life. Wait a minute … let me see that," he said as he grabbed the phone to get a closer look. "Welp, there's your problem," he said handing the phone back to Dave. "You're booked at a different Shoreline Marina in Miami, but that's hours away."

Dave stared at his phone in shock. "You're kidding. I can't believe it. What am I going to do now?"

Margaret rubbed his back. "Hon, we'll figure it out. Call your parents to let them know we're here."

Dave rubbed his hands over his face in frustration. "Well, thank you …"

"Brandon," the guy said as he held out his hand to Dave. "I'm really sorry to see your rental got screwed up. Let me know if I can help find something else in these parts. We've got some nice hotels around here."

Dave shook Brandon's hand and nodded. "Thank you, Brandon. Will do," he said as he dialed his mom's number.

The phone only rang once before Marge's voice burst into the phone's receiver. "Are you guys here?!"

Dave smiled. "We are. Just got here. We're standing on the dock with Brandon."

Marge chuckled. "Oh, you met Brandon. We love him. I'll be right out to grab you two. Have you checked into your boat rental yet?"

Dave sighed heavily. "We'll discuss that mess when we see you guys."

Moments later, Marge and his dad, Roger, came walking down the dock with arms wide open. "So good to see you two. Our first visitors on our boat," Roger said as he and Marge hugged Margaret and Dave.

"So, what's going on with your rental?" Marge asked as she led them down the dock towards their boat.

"I booked it at a marina with the same name in Miami by accident," Dave said with a slight chuckle, grasping to find the humor in the situation.

"Oh, no, that's not good. Guess you're staying here with us," Marge said as they walked onto the boat.

Margaret looked at Dave with widened eyes, then at Marge and Roger. "We don't want to infringe on your space. We can find a nearby hotel."

Dave nodded in agreement. "And there's not much room for us to stay here. It's probably best if we go find a place."

Marge walked straight to the living room couch and pulled it open to reveal a bed. "Look, it already has fresh sheets, waiting just for you. Please stay with us. It will be fun. Find out what it's like to wake up on the water."

Dave glanced at his dad, who shrugged at him, not sure of what his wife was thinking as the boat was pretty cramped with just two people already.

Margaret looked around at how beautifully decorated the boat was on the inside. There were macramé plant hangers hanging from the ceiling with dangling spider plants in them. Sunlight poured through the many windows throughout the place, and the small kitchen was adorable. It had such a lovely, homey feel, she couldn't help but instantly feel enamored with the lifestyle.

"Let's do it," Margaret said as she smiled at Dave. "I think it will be fun."

Dave crossed his arms and looked around the place. "Well, guess we're staying then."

Marge clapped her hands in excitement. "Oh, this is going to be great. I'll make us some lunch. Set your things down and get comfortable."

Dave cleared his throat. "Well, Mom, I was thinking I could take us all out to eat somewhere. Maybe a restaurant on the water?"

Roger laughed and pointed out the window at the water around them. "You can't get closer to the water than here, son."

Dave shrugged and sat down next Margaret, who had already plopped onto the couch and started flipping through a magazine, while Roger sat across from them in "his" chair, and Marge prepared lunch.

"So, how's boat living going?" Dave asked.

Roger clapped his hands together. "It's great. We've made friends with the other folks who live on their boats as well. Some of them are snowbirds like us, and others like to move to different marinas down the coast for variety. We all walk onto each other's boats and talk. It feels almost like roommates since they're so close to us."

Marge grunted as she slathered some mayonnaise on country white bread, then pulled some items out of the small fridge. "Sometimes, I feel I have to whisper for privacy. I once heard every word of what our neighbors next us were talking about the entire evening ... how their daughter was getting a divorce and their son was having his second baby."

Dave rolled his eyes. "Yikes. That sounds a little too close for comfort."

Roger chuckled. "Other than that, it's absolutely wonderful living on a boat."

Marge stopped and put her hand on her hip and stared at Roger. "*Other than that*? How about our toilet situation? That sure gets smelly sometimes … and there always seems to be a project to work on around here, more so than when we lived at the house. Not only that, but we had to put a lot of stuff in storage until we figure out what to do with it because it won't fit on this boat."

Roger shrugged. "Well, we're getting a different toilet system eventually. That'll fix that issue, and it's not so bad being minimalists without *all* that stuff everywhere. It's worth it to wake up right on the water. And the sunsets that come through these windows are miraculous. Wait until you see it this evening," Roger said as he stood up and looked out the window.

Marge eyed the little dining table in the middle of the boat. "Well, enough about that, why don't you all take a seat there. I'm bringing lunch over now."

Roger, Dave, and Margaret took their seats at the table as Marge set down ham and cheese sandwiches cut into fours with a side of bread and butter pickles and a handful of potato chips.

Margaret was starving and immediately dug in, while Dave chuckled. "Mom, you sure haven't changed. This was what we ate for lunch growing up."

Marge took her seat and put her napkin in her lap. "Well, it's still good, right?"

Dave took a bite of his sandwich and swallowed it down with a sip of his Crystal Light iced tea. "It is, Mom. It is … but tonight? I'm treating us to dinner. I don't want to hear otherwise."

* * *

The lunch rush had started at Donna's Restaurant, and Dale was running around with Dixie, one of his managers, helping the busser wipe down tables so the host could seat another party.

Considering patrons had been waiting for a table for thirty

minutes, Dale was none too pleased when he noticed empty drink glasses littering tabletops. He looked over to see the three servers near the bar talking to the bartender and laughing. Dale glanced at Dixie, who had also noticed the servers were slacking.

"I'll handle it," Dixie said as she walked towards the bar to let them know they needed to go check on their tables.

Dale took a breather for a moment and walked to the bar where he kept his bottle of water. Three newly cleaned and set tables had not been sat yet, puzzling him. After walking to the host stand, he found one of their new hosts, Shauna, looking at her phone as guests stood waiting to put their name in.

Frustration grew within Dale, but he kept his cool. "Uh, Shauna?" he asked as he approached the host stand.

Caught off guard, Shauna quickly fumbled with her phone and put it back in her pocket and looked up to see five people standing before her. After proceeding to jot down their names and table sizes, she looked back at Dale. "I'm sorry. I got a text message, and I wasn't aware people were waiting."

Dale sighed. "It's fine, but I prefer the staff to use their phones in the back. I don't want our customers seeing the employees always preoccupied with their phones, ya know?"

Shauna, feeling embarrassed, nodded. "Understood, and I apologize."

"It's all good," Dale said with a smile as he went to go check on some tables.

He walked up to a table with a party of four men in business suits with drinks. "Hi, there. How is everything so far?" Dale asked with a smile.

One of the guys groaned. "We're here on lunch break, and we've been waiting forty minutes for some burgers and sandwiches. I don't think we're going to have time to eat them by the time they get to our table."

Dale's eyes widened. "Oh, no. I'm sorry to hear that. I'll handle this. Let me go see what's going on with your order,"

Dale said as he hurried through the swinging doors into the back of the restaurant.

Once in the kitchen, Dale sensed the chaos. Tickets flew everywhere, people were yelling, pans loudly sizzled, and dishes upon dishes sat in the heating window getting cold as they waited to get run out to tables.

"What's going on back here?" Dale asked, concerned.

Carlos held his hand out from the behind the heating window. "Nobody wants to run this food. We don't have room to put the new food coming out. Where is everyone?"

Dale looked at the tickets quickly and found the four businessmen's orders. He stuck a thermometer in a couple and could tell they were cold already. He tossed them into the closest garbage can. "Carlos, I need you to fire up this ticket's order again. They were cold."

Carolos shook his head in disbelief. "Dale, we need runners back here. Where are the servers? Now we're going to be backed up with everyone else's orders."

Dale sighed and poked his head out of the kitchen's swinging doors to see the servers casually standing around. "We need runners in here," he said to all three servers who then hurried into the kitchen.

Ten minutes later, Dale brought the businessmen their burgers and sandwiches, but by then, they only had ten minutes to eat. "I'm sorry, guys. The bill is on me. We're still working out the kinks after the winter break. I'll bring you some to-go boxes, too," Dale said as he headed to the back again to grab them, while wondering what was going on with his restaurant. It had run so nicely after it opened last year, and now this … whatever this was.

Two hours later, the lunch rush had subsided, and Dale slumped onto a barstool with Dixie seated next to him, looking just as exhausted.

"What happened today? That was a nightmare," Dixie said as she glanced around the now empty restaurant.

Dale shook his head. "I can't figure it out. I guess it's all these new employees not knowing the ropes. Did we not train them well enough?"

Dixie shrugged. "Well, Dale, we don't really have any formal training. We pretty much do a one-day run-through where they shadow another employee in the same position and then … well, then, they start."

Dale sighed. "I guess that way worked all these years for me until now. We're going to have to figure out formal training. Maybe hold weekly meetings prior to the start of lunch and dinner shifts."

Dixie nodded. "I think that sounds like a great idea."

Dale glanced at Dixie who was still all sweaty from running around. "I also think I'm going to need two managers on for lunch shifts, one in the back of the house and one in the front of the house. We're getting too busy during lunch lately, and it's still the off-season. I can't even imagine when it's summertime."

Dixie chuckled. "I have to say, in all my years of restaurant managing, I've never worked with another manager during a lunch shift. I think this great restaurant of yours is growing faster than you expected. That's a good thing."

Dale stood up from his stool. "It is. It sure is, but not if I can't keep up with it. I think I'm going to have our first meeting tomorrow in the kitchen before lunch. I'm going to touch on the fact that if servers aren't busy, they should be running any food in the window. Same for dinner shifts, but I'll also be hiring dedicated food runners to help out. Not only that, but I need to go over cell phone rules, and everything in between."

Dixie gave a sigh of relief. "Glad to hear it. Did you need anything from me before I head out?"

Dale shook his head and smiled. "You've done enough today, Dixie. Go home and relax. I'm going to stay and talk with the kitchen to go over their concerns so I can start coming up with a list of what needs to change in the immediate future. Porridge, my restaurant in Collingswood, never got this busy at lunch. This is a whole new beast for me, and I'm learning as I go, but I really want this restaurant and my employees to succeed."

CHAPTER FIVE

On Sunday morning, the rain poured down outside of the Book Nook as Sarah placed some potted miniature daffodils and fragrant purple hyacinths in the front bay window. She stepped back as she admired her new seasonal window full of novels taking place during the spring and gardening how-to books. She looked around the coffee bar and book shop and took a deep breath, savoring the warm coziness of the place. It smelled like coffee beans, while light, easy listening music played over the speakers. Sarah liked to change up the music daily, but always kept it suitable for working and reading.

"Hey, Sarah, it looks great," Carrie said with a smile as she handed a latte to a customer.

"You think?" Sarah asked her employee as she glanced back at the bay window. "I have some other things to put out, but I'm thinking of making a display on the round wooden table that people can see when they first walk in."

Carrie nodded. "I think that sounds wonderful. Go for it."

Sarah thought for a moment as she walked to the center of the room by the round table, then an idea popped into her head. She came back with the floral teacup and teapot she went back for at West End Garage, placed them on the table, then started walking around the store looking for more spring-themed books.

Suddenly, a clap of thunder made everyone in the shop jump, including Carrie who was just about to hand a black coffee to a man waiting patiently while standing, reading a book. The coffee got all over the counter. "Oh, jeez. Let me get you a new one, sir," she said as she wiped the counter down with a rag.

The man, unfazed, was so deep in his book, he hadn't noticed.

The rain came down even harder as Sarah ran her fingers over the bookshelves, trying to find the perfect books for her display. She stopped when she came to a vintage version of *The Secret Garden*. "This is perfect," she said as she stuffed it into the crook of her arm and continued looking.

The bell on the door started to ring more often as customer after customer came in to get out of the rain, usually stopping to put their umbrellas in the stand by the door, then pausing for a moment to take in the smells and sights of the Book Nook.

Sarah was so enamored with her new business location. The Book Nook, while not as trendy or modern as Monarch Coffeehouse had been, was so nostalgic, wonderful, and cozy. And even now, during a thunderstorm, she couldn't think of anywhere else she'd want to be to enjoy it.

"Sarah," Carrie whispered, causing Sarah to snap out of her thoughts.

"What's up?" Sarah asked as she walked over to the coffee counter.

Carrie motioned with her head to the back reading room, which prompted Sarah to peek in. "What are you showing me?"

Carrie looked back into the room, her eyes landing on a man fully lying down on one of the velvet couches, his head on a throw pillow, asleep with an open book on his chest. "Do you see him?"

Sarah nodded as she stared at the man. "He's been in here every day lately, hasn't he?"

Carrie sighed. "And he's always asleep as though that couch is his bed."

Sarah bit her lip. "He came in when we opened yesterday."

"And he left when we closed at three. He does it almost every day that I'm here," Carrie said, wiping off the counter.

Sarah nodded as she looked back over, watching the paperback book rise and fall with his stomach as he slept soundly even though there were people all around him on chairs, reading and drinking coffee. "He's taking up that entire couch. At least one more person could sit on it comfortably without it being too close for comfort. If he continues this, I'm going to have to say something. Not to mention, it's a little strange for everyone else in the room, no?"

Carrie went to say something, but a loud snore coming from the man startled her, causing her to laugh. "Well, now he's snoring. That is definitely distracting,"

Sarah started walking into the back room, with the intention of waking the man up, but his snores must have beat her to it. He abruptly stopped snoring and sat up, catching the book as it fell to the ground. He then exhaled a deep sigh, opened up the book to exactly where he'd left off, and continued reading like he'd never stopped.

Sarah walked back to the coffee counter and stood next to Carrie. "Well, that saved me an awkward interaction I didn't want to have," she said with a chuckle.

Carrie shook her head and quietly laughed. "I guess we'll see what happens with him. He seems harmless, though." Suddenly a thought popped into her head. "Did you want to try my lavender latte I conjured up this morning? It's delicious. The perfect spring-themed coffee drink."

Sarah nodded. "I would love to. I could use some caffeine right about now."

The front door bell chimed, and in stepped Chris, soaking

wet, looking handsome as ever. Sarah waited for him to notice her, watching him as he glanced around the room. His eyes softened when they landed on her leaning on the counter with a smile.

"Hey. It's a monsoon out there," Chris said as he took off his hat and ran his fingers through his wet hair.

"It sure is. I kind of love it, though. It's such cozy reading weather," Sarah said, glancing out the window. "What are you up to?"

"Well, I've gotta pick up Sam in a little bit, so I was thinking I could swing by and get you for lunch on the way back. You'll be done by then, right?" Chris asked.

Carrie handed Sarah her latte, then nodded at Chris, who nodded back.

Sarah took a sip of her hot drink. "I should be. That sounds great. By the way, did Sam tell you about our run-in with Roberta the other day?"

Chris shook his head. "No. But you didn't either."

Sarah nodded in thought. "You're right. I didn't feel like bringing it up that evening. Didn't think it was important."

Chris paused in thought. "You're bringing it up now, though …."

Sarah looked around the room, then back at Chris. "It was Thursday when Sam and I were shopping at West End Garage right before you took us out for a sunset cruise and dinner. We were killing time, and there was Roberta, out of nowhere."

"OK … Did you talk? What happened?" Chris asked.

"Well, let's just say she had a lot to say. For one—" Sarah stopped as she noticed some customers seemed to be listening to the whole conversation. "You know what, let's talk about this another time."

Chris held his hands up, confused. "Well, now I want to know what she said."

Just then, the bell chimed on the door, and three customers walked in and stood at the counter, browsing the coffee menu.

Sarah walked towards Chris as Carrie got to work taking and making orders. "Look, I made a mistake bringing it up here. We'll talk about it later."

All of a sudden, a loud clap of thunder made everyone in the Book Nook jump, followed by the pounding downpour of rain on the roof.

Chris moved a piece of hair off of Sarah's face, then quickly kissed her forehead. "Well, so be it. I've gotta go get Sam. I'll give you call when we're on our way back."

* * *

Loud noises exploded from the kitchen as Donna closed the door of the bedroom, then flopped on her bed, slipping on her padded headphones. She leaned back against the bed's head-board and opened her laptop to start reading.

Bang, bang, bang.

Donna whipped off her headphones and stared at the door just as her phone rang.

"Dale, what's up?" Donna answered.

Dale sighed. "A little of this and a lot of that. It's nuts here at the restaurant."

Donna sighed too. "Sorry to hear. It's also nuts around the house. I have this huge test tonight in my class, and I can't get in any of my studying. It's so loud, I can hear everything through my headphones. It's so distracting."

Dale felt his heart sink for her. "Why don't you go to a coffee shop or something?"

Donna thought for a moment. "But we need someone to be here. We don't really know these guys *that* well. They might leave with the door unlocked or who knows what."

Dale chuckled. "Donna, it's fine. I'll be home in a few hours. Just get out of the house so you can study."

Donna nodded and shut her laptop. "OK, I've got an idea. I'm going to sit in in my car in the driveway."

Dale shrugged and some loud clangs came from the restaurant's kitchen. "OK, whatever works for you. I've got to go see what that noise was."

Donna laughed. "Guess we're both trying to work with loud noises, huh?"

Dale smiled. "You could say that. OK, gorgeous. I'll see you soon. Go study so you'll ace this test."

Donna hung up and stood from the bed. She picked up her laptop and purse, then stepped outside to a now sunny sky. After raining all morning, the weather had shifted finally. She opened her car door, hopped into the front seat, rolled down some of the windows halfway, then opened her laptop to start reading.

Fifteen minutes into taking notes and studying, the noises from the kitchen remodel spread outside. She quickly rolled up the windows and turned the radio on.

"That's better," she said as she nestled in, realizing she liked this method of studying.

Five minutes later, some workers stepped out of the house, carting the old kitchen island countertop and headed towards her car.

Donna rolled her window down. "Do you need me to move?"

"Yes, that would be great. We need to get to that dumpster behind you," one of the workers said. "It's too wide to fit past."

Donna closed her laptop, started the car's engine, and pulled it out of the driveway. Once in the middle of the street, she quickly realized there wasn't anywhere close to park since all of the work vehicles were taking up the extra curb space. She made a split-second decision to drive to one of the benches at Lily Lake.

A few minutes later, she was parked and sitting on the bench by the lake on a warm, sunny spring day. She cracked her knuckles and opened her laptop.

Two hours had passed of undistracted notecard writing

and textbook reading when Donna heard some splashing noises. She looked over to see a family of swans—Mom, Dad, and four babies—swimming right next to her.

Feeling satisfied with her studying, Donna closed her laptop, and watched the swan family swim happily together. She stood up from the bench, and walked closer to the lake, noticing a handful of turtles sunning themselves on a log, and in the water, she saw tiny fish. Spring had definitely sprung, and it sure made her happy.

Donna headed back to her car, got in, and placed her laptop on the passenger seat. Before starting the engine, she took one last look at the lake. Why didn't she visit such a beautiful oasis more often? It was not far from their house, either. Perhaps that ocean in their backyard had stolen all the attention. Not anymore. She was ready to explore every little nook and cranny their town offered, and she wanted Dale to come too.

* * *

Margaret, Dave, Roger, and Marge all sat on the sand together in sunny Daytona, Florida under beach umbrellas.

"Isn't this great? You can drive your four-wheel drive right onto the beach here. No dragging your beach items blocks away from the car," Roger said as he leaned back in his very old-school beach chair that sat close to the ground.

Margaret nodded as she watched the waves crash ahead of them. "I guess it is nice. Feels like we're the only ones out here too."

Marge sighed. "It does, doesn't it? Makes me miss my Jersey beaches. Can't get lonely there," she said with a chuckle.

Roger sat up from his chair and looked Marge square in the face. "You mean to tell me you *like* having hundreds of people all up in your space?"

Dave laughed, knowing full well his mother would always

be a Jersey girl at heart and his dad, well, he'd already pledged his allegiance to Florida, it seemed.

Marge stared back at Roger and took off her sunglasses. "Yes, that's what I'm saying. I like it. I like seeing my grandkids make friends. I like people watching. Frankly, I like the extra company."

Roger shook his head in disbelief and faced the ocean again. "Well, Marge, did you tell Dave and Margaret the news?"

Marge shook her head. "I haven't."

Margaret and Dave looked at each other with widened eyes. "What news?" Dave asked, feeling anxiety creep in. Hopefully, they were still staying married after the fiftieth anniversary fiasco.

"We're coming home a month early. We'll be back in Jersey in time for Easter. I can't wait," Marge said as she applied sunblock to her arms.

Dave paused in thought. "Mom, that's this coming weekend. It's six days away. When are you two planning to leave Florida?"

Roger sighed. "It'll take four or five days to get there by boat if we stop every night, so we're planning to leave Tuesday and getting there by Saturday."

Margaret clapped her hands. "That's great. My parents are hosting a big Easter dinner this year. I'm sure they have room for more. Would you want to come?"

Marge smiled from ear to ear. "We'd love that. Tell Judy, I'll bring a seven-layer salad. I can't wait to be back in my home state."

Roger shrugged and opened his magazine. "Well, you know me, I'd rather be in Florida."

Marge waved him off, then took a sip of her drink that sat in her chair's cupholder. "We found a nice marina in Cape May to dock at. I've already got plans with friends and family lined up. We were waiting to tell you two when you arrived."

Dave bit his lip. "What's Mike doing for Easter? Will he and his family be around? Haven't talked to him in a bit."

Roger put his magazine down. "Your brother? He said they're going to his in-laws this Easter."

Dave smiled and glanced at Margaret. "You probably should text your mom about my parents coming so she knows."

"Oh, I'll give her a call later. It'll be fine. She always loves having a lot of people over," Margaret said as she reclined back in her chair, trying to savor their last day in Florida.

CHAPTER SIX

Early the next morning, Judy and Bob were back on board the Cape May-Lewes Ferry enjoying the same seats on the upper deck that they had before.

"This hot coffee is hitting the spot right now," Judy said as she took a sip and smiled while she looked out towards the water.

Bob drank some of his coffee, then sat back in his chair and closed his eyes, letting the light breeze, sound of the seagulls, and lapping water whisk him to his happy place. "You know, I'm glad we came back to do this again. I really enjoy being on the ferry."

Judy smiled. "It is nice, isn't it? I think we may have broken that ferry curse we had going there," she said with a chuckle.

Bob nodded. "Our last trip the other day was perfect. Every part of it. We surely have. Maybe we can make this a monthly thing."

Judy laughed. "You like it that much, eh?"

Bob shrugged. "I mean, I'm fine if we just ride the ferry back and forth and don't get off the boat at all. I like being on the water."

Judy took a deep happy sigh as the boat approached their

destination. "Don't get too comfortable. Looks like we're here already."

Bob sat up and finished his coffee. "That was quick. Time flies when you're enjoying life," he said as they watched the boat pull in.

Fifteen minutes later, they were driving off the ferry while Judy sat in the passenger seat looking at the GPS on her phone. "Make a left here. This road should take us straight to Cape Henlopen State Park," Judy said.

Bob glanced up at the sky as he drove. "Looks like the rain is holding off for now. Hopefully, we can get in a good bit of walking before it starts."

Judy nodded. "That's why I'm glad we're here nice and early. I've always wanted to stroll Gordon's Pond Trail."

Bob looked in the rearview mirror at the other cars that had been behind him. "Looks like we weren't the only ones on the ferry who had this idea," he said as he pulled into a parking space.

They got out of the car and started walking on the trail.

"Oh, wow. Look at the blue heron flying over the pond, Bob," Judy said as they approached a platform.

Bob walked to the railing just as a bicyclist came flying around the corner and almost crashed into him. Bob jumped back out of the way, feeling his heart race. "This also for walkers, right?"

Judy bit her lip as she watched more and more bikers fly by them, feeling like maybe this wasn't meant to be a walking path. Then, a group of walkers appeared from around the bend, and she breathed a deep sigh of relief. "Looks like it. We aren't the only ones not on a bike it seems."

Bob looked at his watch. "Well, are you ready to get going again? I'd like to get my ten-thousand steps in today. I've only got about a thousand so far."

Judy smiled. "I'm so glad you're working on your health."

After finishing the three-plus-mile loop around the pond,

Bob paused a moment, while Judy continued walking towards the parking lot.

"Where are you going?" Bob asked. "I'm just getting warmed up. I need another five thousand steps."

Judy wiped the sweat from her brow. "Bob, I'm tired and hungry. How about we head out for something to eat."

Bob made a sad face. "You sure you don't want to go around the pond one more time?"

Judy sighed while walking towards Bob. "Fine, but let's make this quick."

Twenty minutes of speed walking later, Bob abruptly started limping and moaning. "I've got a charley horse. My calf is killing me," he said, holding his leg and wincing in pain.

Judy studied his calf. "Oh, no. We've got another mile to go until we get to the car, Bob. Do you want to find somewhere to sit and rest for a bit?"

Bob shook his head. "No. I'm going to push through. Look, the sky is turning gray. That rain is coming."

They started walking, but Bob found that he couldn't walk very fast without being in pain. So, slowly, he hobbled as best he could on the path back.

"We're almost to the car, Bob," Judy said after thirty minutes.

Bob stopped and looked at the sky just as tiny raindrops started falling on them. "It's starting to rain. We've got to hurry," he said. No sooner had they taken a dozen strides than the skies opened up, unleashing a torrential downpour.

Judy spotted the car one hundred feet away in the parking lot. "Bob, I'm making a run for it."

Bob did a hobble skip behind her until they were both back in the car, panting and watching the rain pelt down all around them.

"Just let me sit here for three hours," Bob said half-jokingly as he leaned his head back on the passenger's seat headrest.

Judy chuckled as she took over driving. "We're heading to

Matt's Fish Camp. Linda and I ate there once one years ago, and it was incredible."

Bob laughed as he realized something. "I don't think we broke the ferry curse after all, dear. We're both soaking wet, and my calf still hurts."

Judy shrugged and chuckled. "Well, you may be right about that. The ferry adventure curse lives on. We'll have to come back and try to break it again."

Fifteen minutes later, they pulled up to the restaurant and were promptly seated inside.

Judy looked over the menu, trying to figure out what she wanted to eat, when her phone rang. "Oh, it's Margaret. They must be home from Florida," Judy said as she answered.

"Hey, Mom," Margaret said as Dave drove them back to Cape May from the airport.

"Hi, Margaret! You guys landed? Was your flight good?" Judy asked.

"It was great. No turbulence and I was even able to get some work done," Margaret said with a smile.

"Oh, that's wonderful. Well, we took the ferry to Delaware after we dropped the girls off at school this morning. Liz offered to pick them up after school for us in case you weren't home in time," Judy said.

"Oh, that won't be necessary. I'll let Liz know I can get them," Margaret said as she glanced at Dave.

"Did you guys have a nice trip? Oh, hold on, Margaret," Judy said as their server approached. "I have to order my food and drink. We're at a restaurant." Moments later, Judy was back on the phone. "OK, I'm done. Where were we?"

"Well, our trip was nice. Didn't go exactly as planned, as Dave accidentally booked our houseboat rental in Miami and not Daytona," Margaret said with a chuckle.

Dave shook his head and laughed as he drove. "Don't remind me."

Margaret continued on, "We mainly spent time with his

49

parents on their boat and on the beach. We went out to dinner. You know, all that stuff. I think his parents were so glad to have us there. By the way, they're going to be here for Easter. I told them they could come to dinner at your house. I'm assuming that's OK?"

Judy nodded happily. "Yes, it'll be great to have them on Easter. You know, the more the merrier."

Bob looked at Judy with confusion on his face. "*More* people are coming to Easter?"

"Yes, Dave's parents will be in town. Won't it be nice to have them over?" Judy asked.

Bob widened his eyes. "At this point, we need to rent out the VFW. Where are we going to put all these people?"

Margaret overheard the conversation. "Mom, do you want us to host Easter? We have more space at our place."

Now Dave was looking at Margaret with confusion. "How are you going to do that while handling the brunch and Easter festivities at the Seahorse?"

Margaret shrugged.

"Nonsense. I want Easter at our house," Judy said matter-of-factly. "We haven't hosted Easter in years, and I miss it. I'm excited to have everyone over. We'll figure something out, whether we put some tables and chairs outside or what have you. We'll make it work. Everyone is welcome."

Bob rolled his eyes, knowing Judy was biting off more than she could chew at this point.

"Well, OK, Mom. Let me and Liz know what we can do to help. I think we have extra chairs we can bring over and probably some folding tables," Margaret said as they approached the parkway.

"Will do. Drive safely and give me a call later," Judy said as she hung up the phone.

Margaret put her phone in her purse then sighed deeply as she stared ahead at the road.

"Everything OK?" Dave asked.

Margaret nodded. "I think so. I can already tell it's going to be a chaotic Easter weekend."

* * *

Around three that afternoon, Margaret dashed through the rain into the Seahorse Inn with Abby and Harper behind her.

"What are you all cooking? It smells wonderful," Margaret said as she hung her wet jacket on the coat rack.

Liz walked out of the kitchen holding a dish with potholders. "Baked apple oatmeal, right out of the oven. Would you guys like to try some? Just testing items for brunch this weekend."

Margaret nodded. "I'd love to have some. How about you two?" she asked Harper and Abby.

Harper shook her head. "I don't like oatmeal. Can I go watch a movie in the basement?"

Abby shrugged. "I'll try some of it, but I want to go in the basement too."

Margaret sighed. "OK, you two. I'll bring down some food in a bit. Don't forget to get your homework done too."

Abby and Harper rushed towards the basement door, swung it open, and stampeded down the carpeted steps to the spiffy drive-in-movie-theater-style room.

Liz scooped some of the oatmeal onto a plate and handed it to Margaret with a fork.

Margaret leaned on the kitchen island while taking a bite. "Oh, this is good. Really good. By the way, where's everyone else?"

Liz pointed upstairs as she chewed. "Jackie, Irene, and Bonnie are upstairs cleaning, and Dolly and Kim went grocery shopping for this weekend."

Margaret bit her lip. "No guests?"

Liz shook her head. "The last guests left this morning.

We're empty until Friday, and then we're completely booked all weekend.

Margaret nodded. "Well, I guess we should figure out if we need another table? We also have to work on logistics for the Easter egg hunt."

Suddenly, the front door swung open, and Dolly and Kim lugged in four bags each of groceries.

"Here, let me help," Margaret said as she took two bags from Dolly.

Liz grabbed two bags from Kim, and they all walked into the kitchen together.

Dolly took a breather as she looked towards the front window, watching the rain come down. "I've never seen anything like this rain. I know it's April, but my goodness, it hasn't let up!"

Margaret nodded in agreement as she put groceries away.

When the inn's phone rang, Kim said, "I'll get it," and she picked up the receiver. "Hello, Seahorse Inn."

"Hello, there. This is Maxine Brown. We're just confirming our reservation for this weekend."

Kim opened the reservation book, then leafed through it until she got to Easter weekend, where she ran her finger down the page. "Maxine Brown ... I don't see that name here. Could you have possibly made the reservation under a different name?"

Maxine shook her head. "No, it was in my name. I booked five rooms for my large family last fall."

Kim bit her lip. "Hold on, Maxine. Let me look into this," she said as she put the phone on mute.

"Guys, we may have a problem. I have Maxine Brown on the phone who says she booked five rooms for this weekend months ago. She's not on the books, and there aren't any rooms available," Kim said.

Margaret shook her head. "I don't remember taking a

reservation for a Maxine Brown. Do any of you?" she asked as Irene, Jackie, and Bonnie walked into the kitchen together.

The ladies shook their heads, confirming they hadn't taken the reservation, while Liz sheepishly raised her hand. "I think it may have been me."

"Really?" Margaret asked. "Did you forget to write it in?"

Liz nodded. "I totally forgot about this until now, but she called right before I was leaving to pick the boys up from school. I wasn't even supposed to be here that day. I'd stopped in to drop something off and decided to take the call. There wasn't anything to write on, so I thought I'd just text one of you later on, and I guess I never did."

Margaret rubbed her hand over her face, feeling anxiety creep in. "What are we going to do?"

Kim shrugged. "I guess we'll tell her there's been a horrible mix-up with the reservations, and we can no longer accommodate them?"

Margaret shook her head. "We can't do that. How devastating. Tell her we'll see her and her family this weekend."

Liz's eyes widened. "Where are we going to put them? Our own houses? We're fully booked."

Margaret deeply sighed as she walked to the front door and swung it open, revealing the pouring rain. She stepped out onto the porch with Liz following behind her. There she stood, looking up and down Beach Avenue at the many houses and B&Bs.

"What are you thinking?" Liz asked.

"We're going to have to figure something out for them," Margaret said as she walked back inside and picked up the phone. "Maxine?" Margaret asked.

"Hi, yes, this is her," Maxine said.

"Hi, I'm Margaret. I'm one of the owners of the Seahorse Inn. Your reservation, mistakenly, was never put in the books."

"Oh, no," Maxine said, tears welling up in her eyes.

"Don't get upset. I'm going to figure something out for you

and your family. Still plan on coming to the Seahorse Inn," Margaret said as she looked at the confusion on all of the ladies' faces in the room.

"But how is that going to work? Where will we stay?" Maxine asked.

Margaret nodded. "I have some ideas up my sleeve that I think might work. I'm friends with other B&B owners near me. I will make sure you have somewhere just as nice to stay and you can still be a part of the Easter brunch and festivities here at the Seahorse Inn with your relatives."

Maxine breathed a sigh of relief, though still felt uneasy at the thought of not knowing exactly where they'd be staying. "Thank you. It's much appreciated."

CHAPTER SEVEN

Liz stood in kitchen looking through an old recipe book she'd had forever. She was in the mood to cook a new type of dinner this evening but didn't have a clue as to what.

She picked up her phone and dialed Margaret.

"Hello?" Margaret answered.

"Hey, birthday girl! Happy birthday!" Liz said.

"Thank you, Liz! I'm still doing fundraising work at home for the wildlife refuge. Dave's picking the girls up from school, then we're going to go out."

"Oh, where to?" Liz asked as her front door opened and her sons walked in, followed by Hailey and Jamie again.

"I was thinking maybe Ocean City."

Liz watched as the boys waved to her, then headed straight for the back door, walking outside with the girls behind them.

Liz lost track of the conversation. "That sounds great. The boys just got in. They've been hanging out with these two girls lately, and they came home with them again. Anyway, I hope you enjoy the rest of your day."

Margaret sighed. "I'll try. I'm not letting myself stress about the Seahorse."

Liz smacked her head. "That's right. I was swamped with

work in my office all day. I haven't had a second to contact anyone. Have you heard about any availability at other nearby B&Bs for Maxine?"

Margaret shook her head. "I called ten places. Everybody is booked."

Liz bit her lip. "What about the Morning Dew Cottage? Hugh and Betty? Are they booked?"

"I haven't heard back from them yet. In fact, I haven't seen them around at all. Have you?" Margaret asked.

Liz paused in thought. "You know, I haven't. I figured since we're only there every so often, maybe we keep missing them. Once I figure out dinner, I'll try and call a few places."

Margaret smiled. "That'd be great. Thank you."

Liz looked outside to see Michael and Steven playing some sort of tackle football with Hailey and Jamie. She smiled. "OK, well I'll talk to you later. Have fun in Ocean City."

They said their goodbyes, and Liz tried to look through her recipes once more but couldn't help but watch her sons outside. She wasn't used to seeing them with friends that were girls. It was almost as if they were flirting ….

She was startled by her phone ringing.

"Hey, Greg," Liz answered.

"Hey. Just checking in. Making sure everything is good at the house," Greg said with a smile.

Liz looked outside. "Well, I guess it is. The boys brought over Hailey and Jamie again. It's really nice seeing them have some friends that are of the opposite sex, isn't it?"

Greg laughed. "*Friends?*"

Liz shifted her eyes. "Yes, *friends*. Margaret and I both had our fair share of friends that were male growing up."

Greg laughed. "You *thought* they were friends. They thought at any moment it could be something more."

Liz shook her head. "That's not true."

"Oh, really? Well, when you got a boyfriend, were these male friends still in the picture?" Greg asked.

Liz thought for a moment. "Not really."

"Exactly," Greg said, feeling proud of himself.

Liz walked towards the fridge and glanced at the calendar hanging on the wall. "Oh! By the way, I forgot to tell you, we're chaperoning Michael and Steven's spring dance this Friday. You said you were off that day, so I signed you up."

Greg chuckled as he sat at a table in the wine cellar portion of the restaurant. "Ah, the good ol' spring fling. Should be a good time," he said as he watched Dale walk in and pull up a seat at his table.

Liz nodded. "I'm excited. OK, I'll let you get back to work. By the way, I'm making dinner tonight if you want leftovers when you get home."

"Sounds good. Dale just showed up, so I'm going to talk with him," Greg said as they both hung up.

Greg put his phone on the table in the dimly lit room and nodded at Dale. "No offense, but you look absolutely exhausted."

Dale leaned back in his chair and ran his fingers through his hair. "I feel exhausted. Donna's isn't running like it was before the winter break. It feels like the place is slowly falling apart."

Greg nodded. "I've been there with this place. Did you just finish the lunch shift?"

Dale sighed. "Yep, and it's getting busier every day. Last year in the off-season, lunches were pretty slow. So much so I considered only being open for dinner like you here at Heirloom ... but I can't imagine what summer will be like if it's like this in April."

Greg smiled. "I'm impressed. I'm sure you'll work the kinks out."

Dale shook his head. "I haven't told anyone this yet, but I think one of my employees is stealing money from the restaurant."

Greg's eyes widened. "Who?"

Dale shrugged and held up his hands. "I wish I knew."

"You've got cameras, right?" Greg asked.

Dale sighed. "Just one outside facing the street and one in the front of the restaurant."

Greg nodded. "I'd look into installing a few more. It can't hurt, right? How did you figure out this was happening?"

Dale paused in thought. "The money drawer has been coming up short ever since we reopened whenever I counted it before leaving for the day. At first, it was just five dollars here or there, and I thought nothing of it. Then, this past week, it was a hundred dollars short one day, and three hundred the next. Then today, before I left? Five hundred. Something is going on."

Greg leaned back in his chair in thought and stretched his arms behind his head. "I would probably think the same thing. Thankfully, I haven't had that issue here. Did it ever happen over at Porridge?"

"Nope. Never. I think maybe once or twice the money drawer was short a few dollars, but that's usually attributed to miscalculation or something, you know?" Dale said as he racked his brain.

Greg sat up and leaned on the table. "Well, who has access to the money drawer? I imagine not everyone?"

"Me, the managers, the bartender, the servers if they need to make change ..."

Greg shook his head. "First things first. Install a camera near wherever the money drawer is. Secondly, I would only allow you and the managers access to the money drawer."

Dale sighed. "You're right, and I should know better. I've been running restaurants for years. I guess I've always been very trusting of my employees and never had to worry about things like this. Heck, I never had a reason to worry until now."

Greg reached over and patted Dale on the shoulder. "I'm

always here if you need any help. We can help each other, ya know?"

Dale smiled. "Thank you, Greg. It means the world to have a friend like you. By the way, are you still doing Easter brunch this Sunday?"

Greg rolled his eyes and sighed. "I was … but I only have three, yes *three*, reservations for Sunday."

Dale nodded. "Did you post about it on social media?"

Greg shook his head. "Nah, I don't do social media. Once in a while, Liz will post something for me on Heirloom's page, but that's about it."

Dale sighed. "Well, that's your problem. Everyone knows you're only a dinner restaurant, so how's anyone supposed to know you're offering brunch on Sunday?"

"You're right. You're absolutely right. The question is is it too late now? Maybe we should just cancel the brunch at this point."

* * *

At 3 p.m., Dave, Margaret, Harper, and Abby drove up the parkway, ready for Margaret's birthday adventure.

Dave looked over at Margaret and smiled. "So, are you sure this is where you want to spend your birthday? Ocean City?"

Margaret shrugged. "Yes. I haven't been to Ocean City in some time. I miss it."

Dave nodded and turned up the seventies rock that was playing on the radio. "Well, Ocean City it is."

Harper and Abby quietly worked on homework in the back seat, while Margaret happily looked out the window. Thirty-five minutes or so later, they finally crossed the 9th Street bridge into Ocean City.

Dave found an empty parking lot off of 9th, directly next to the boardwalk, parked the truck, and they all got out.

"Looks like we've got a nice warm day without rain. Perfect for walking the boards," Dave said as he looked up at the sky.

Margaret smiled as she put her arms around Harper and Abby. "Anyone hungry? I'm craving some Manco & Manco Pizza. You know it's my favorite."

Harper and Abby ran up the ramp to the boardwalk, then turned back to watch Dave and Margaret walk up behind them. "We're starving. I want three slices of plain," Abby said.

Margaret laughed. "We'll get a table and a pie to share," she said as she opened the door and stepped inside the delicious-smelling pizza shop.

After ordering and getting their drinks, the hot pie finally arrived.

Dave picked up his slice from his paper plate, folded it, and took a big bite. "This is the best pizza."

Margaret nodded as she took a bite of her slice. "It is. You know, I've been thinking. That guest, Maxine, that booked five rooms with us for Easter weekend and it was never put in our reservation book? I told her I would find somewhere for her and her family to stay …."

"Did you find a place?" Dave asked.

Margaret shook her head. "Nobody's getting back to me. I'm starting to get nervous. Do you think I could put them up in the beach house?"

Dave's eyes widened. "I don't think that would work. It's only three bedrooms, and the faucet in the bathroom still doesn't work. My plumber can't come out until next weekend."

Margaret took a sip of her birch beer and sighed. "Yeah, that won't work. Maybe we can put them up in our house or Liz and Greg's?"

Dave shook his head and chuckled. "We don't have five bedrooms, and I don't think Liz and Greg would be down for that either."

Margaret nodded. "You're right," she said as she looked

over to see Abby and Harper getting ready to eat their second slices. "Wow, you two are pretty hungry."

Abby smiled. "I told you I wanted three slices, remember?"

Harper nodded in agreement. "I want three too."

Margaret looked at the one slice left in the pie. "Guess we're ordering another pizza," she said with a chuckle.

After finishing the second pizza, they all walked over to get ice cream at Kohr Brothers Frozen Custard. After everyone ordered, Margaret was the last up. "I'll have a peanut butter and chocolate twist on a waffle cone with rainbow sprinkles," she said to the guy working the frozen custard stand.

The guy picked up a waffle cone, then walked to a custard machine behind him, and pulled down the lever. Out came a swirly mix of custard, which was then rolled in a bin of colorful sprinkles and handed to Margaret.

Margaret took a bite and savored it as she watched Dave, Harper, and Abby enjoying theirs. "This is heaven. I wish it was healthy to eat this stuff every day."

Dave laughed and looked down the long boardwalk. "Well, we can walk some of these calories off, that's for sure."

They walked a bit, enjoying the ocean breeze, while looking at some of the shops that had opened for the spring season.

Harper pointed up. "Look! The Ferris wheel is working. Can we go on it?"

Margaret shrugged. "We just ate a lot of food. Are you sure you want to do that?"

Harper and Abby nodded excitedly.

Dave smiled at Margaret. "Come on. Let's do it. The Ferris wheel doesn't go too fast."

Margaret sighed. "Alright. Fine. Ferris wheel it is, then."

Ten minutes later, they were in a pod together on the Ferris wheel as they started moving to the top, where it stopped.

Margaret nervously glanced around. "Why are we stopped?"

Dave looked down. "Oh, they're just letting people off and getting new people on."

Margaret gave a sigh of relief as Harper and Abby looked out towards the boardwalk at the people walking.

"Is that Dad?" Harper yelled.

Abby squinted her eyes to get a better look. "I think so. Isn't that Katie?"

Harper nodded. "Oh, yeah. That's probably who that is."

Margaret and Dave cocked their heads to see, then Margaret widened her eyes. "Who's Katie, and is she pregnant?" she quietly said to Dave.

Abby overheard her. "Yes. Her and Dad are having a baby. We told you, don't you remember?"

Margaret was taken aback. "I'm sorry. I don't remember hearing anything about Katie. What a—"

"Nice surprise," Dave said, filling in her sentence for her before things became awkward around the girls. "So, you two are going to both be big sisters now. That's exciting."

The girls shrugged. "I guess," Abby said. "I actually prefer being the baby of the family, though."

Margaret was still deep in thought, but she snapped out of it quickly and put her arm around Abby. "Well, you'll always be our baby."

Abby smiled and hugged Dave and Margaret while Harper waved and screamed trying to get Paul's attention, but they were too far away.

The Ferris wheel started moving again, and this time a lot more quickly than Margaret remembered. She grabbed Dave's arm as she braced herself against the seat, feeling her stomach turn.

"You OK?" Dave asked as he grabbed Margaret's hand in his.

"I'm starting to think this Ferris wheel was a bad idea right after eating," Margaret said, knowing full well it was a mix of that and finding out her ex-husband was going to be a father again. Something about it just didn't sit right with her. How long had he been with that woman? Did they live together? Would Paul have less time for the girls once he had another child? Was Katie nice to the girls?

Within moments, the Ferris wheel stopped, and they were walking out of their pod and back onto the boardwalk where Margaret took a deep breath and pulled Dave in for a big hug.

Dave hugged her back. "Do you want to go home?"

Margaret shook her head, then looked out towards the ocean. "I think we should all take our shoes off and walk on the beach. I need some sand and ocean therapy right now."

The girls ran ahead onto a bench where they slipped off their shoes while Dave pulled Margaret aside.

"Does this whole Paul thing bother you?" Dave asked, concern growing on his face.

Margaret sighed. "It's more how it will affect the girls, you know? It's kind of a big deal, especially for them. They're going to have another sibling."

Dave nodded and kissed her on her head. "It is. You're right, but it's out of our hands. It will all work out, I'm sure. Let's forget this and enjoy ourselves," he said as he took his shoes off.

CHAPTER EIGHT

Judy walked around Cape Island Gardens looking at all the potted Easter flowers. She stopped and smelled some bright-pink hyacinths and smiled as she looked around at all of the beautiful plants for sale. She walked over towards a shed and peeked in to see decorative pots for sale when her phone rang from her purse. She reached in and picked it up

"Hello?" Judy answered.

"Judy, it's Carol," her sister said as she watched her grand-kids work on a puzzle in the living room.

"Oh, my lovely sister. How *good* to hear from you," Judy said, half teasing.

Carol rolled her eyes. "We spoke a week and a half ago. You act like I never call," she joked.

Judy stepped out of the shed and touched a lush green hanging fern in front of her. "Well, how are things?"

Carol cleared her throat. "Things are good … I'm guessing you heard that Linda and I aren't speaking currently."

Judy stopped in her tracks. "Well, yes, I did hear that. Why don't you two patch things up. This is getting silly."

Carol sighed. "Have you even heard *my* side of the story?"

Judy shrugged. "No, but do I need to? I'm not taking sides.

I just want you all to be on good terms by this weekend for Easter."

Carol cut in. "Well, I admit, I did go a little overboard on Linda, but this isn't the first time she's forgotten something like this. Not even two weeks prior she forgot our breakfast date. I get to the diner, text her that I'm there, and nothing. I ended up eating my two eggs over easy with home fries and toast by myself. I called a few times, but it went straight to voice mail. She's always turning that cell phone off when she's not using it. What's the point of even having one?"

Judy walked by some flats of colorful impatiens and thought for a moment. "That's odd."

Carol nodded in agreement. "It is, isn't it? That's not all. A month ago, she was supposed to drive me to my doctor's appointment. My car was in the shop, and Jack was out helping a friend move, and I didn't want to bother my kids since they all work full-time jobs, so I called Linda. I texted her and called the morning of to remind her, but her phone was turned off. I didn't end up making that appointment, and I didn't hear from Linda until the next morning when she finally turned her phone on."

Judy shook her head. "What about Linda's landline?"

Carol laughed. "They got rid of that earlier in the year since Mike and her mainly use their cell phones now. There wasn't any way to get ahold of her. What if there had been an emergency?"

Judy shrugged. "Well, in that case, you could always call Mike."

"True, but then Mike is usually out and about and not at home. Linda needs to come to her senses. It's getting out of hand," Carol said.

Judy laughed. "You could have emailed her. Sorry, just thinking of ways to get in touch with Linda."

Carol shook her head and chuckled. "Oh, yeah right! She

never responds to emails. Good luck getting ahold of her that way."

Judy nodded "Well, that leaves us at a messenger pigeon."

Carol laughed. "That might be our only option left."

Judy nodded. "Well, we'll all talk at Easter. You're still coming, right?"

Carol chuckled. "Of course. Wouldn't miss it for the world, even if my sister is driving me nuts. Doesn't she have a calendar that she writes stuff down on? I just can't understand how she can be so forgetful. Anyway, what do you need me to bring on Sunday?"

Judy headed back to the potted hyacinths, daffodils, and tulips. "Well, I'm picking out potted flower centerpieces for the tables now, but I think it's going to be a good amount of people this year. Bring whatever you want. I'm sure it will get eaten."

Carol paused in thought. "I'll bring my pineapple stuffing and dessert, not sure what kind yet, though. Does that work? By the way, how's Bob doing?"

Judy smiled. "That works great, and Bob is doing well. He's actually out walking. It's his new thing these days."

Carol's eyes widened. "Bob? Really? I'm surprised you're not out walking with him."

Judy looked at the potted daffodils and tulips she was about to buy. "Well, I had some things I needed to do, but I do enjoy it. Probably next time. Well, we'll talk soon. I've got to get going," Judy said. With that, they said their goodbyes, and she paid for the flowers.

* * *

While Judy loaded her purchases into her car's trunk, Bob was getting his steps in over on the Cape May Promenade. He was about a mile in of walking when an old high school classmate jogged right past, then stopped and walked back towards him.

"Bob?" the guy asked.

"Tim? I thought that was you," Bob said as he shook Tim's hand and smiled. "How've you been?"

Tim, who was also in his seventies, pulled his shirt up over his face and wiped the sweat off, revealing a somewhat chiseled looking chest and abs. "I'm doing great. Never felt better. I'm trying to get in a fifteen-mile jog today."

Bob laughed. "I'm impressed. I've just started seriously walking, you know, getting those ten thousand steps in that everyone is doing."

"Oh yeah? That's great. When you want to work up to a jog, let me know. I could use another local running partner," Tim said as he looked out towards the ocean.

Bob chuckled. "That might be a while. I've never been a big exerciser, so even all this walking is relatively new to me, but you look amazing … even healthier and more fit than back in high school."

Tim walked over to a nearby bench to stretch his leg. "Well, it's not all only from jogging. I've been into strength training the last five years, and it's been transformative for both my body and mind. I spend around two hours a day in the gym. It's become quite the lifestyle."

Bob looked down at his gut and took a deep breath. "Well, I'm really happy for you. You're definitely inspiring, Tim."

Tim took a deep breath, then looked at his phone. "Here, take down my number in case you ever want to come join me."

Bob fumbled with his phone in his pocket, then put in Tim's number under his contacts. "Well, it was nice running into you. See you around," Bob said.

Tim jogged off, then turned back to wave. "Take care, Bob. Keep at those exercise goals."

Bob went back to walking, feeling inspired by Tim's dedication. Maybe he could work up to a jog someday. Maybe just maybe he could try a light jog now ….

Looking down at the pedometer on his phone, he popped in his headphones, turned on an audiobook, and started walking even faster until he was at a slow jog. He felt the ocean breeze on his face and the sun on his skin, and it felt wonderful.

Suddenly his calf cramped up again, causing a shooting pain up his leg. He hobbled to a bench and called Judy.

"Hi, dear," Judy answered as she stepped out of her car in the driveway.

"You in the car?" Bob asked.

"Just got out. Why is that?" Judy answered.

"I need you to come pick me up near Broadway on the Promenade. Got another charley horse calf cramp," Bob said, wincing from the pain.

"Again?" Judy asked.

"Yep. Second time it's happened since I started this walking. I decided to try and jog this time around, and it came back," Bob said as he rubbed his leg.

Judy chuckled and shook her head. "Jog? I'd put in more walking hours before you try jogging, hon. I'm on my way to get you. Hold tight."

Bob ended the call and stood up to stretch his leg on the bench, feeling the cramp start to subside. Suddenly, it dawned on him. He hadn't been doing any stretching before or after his walks like he should have been. Heck, it had been probably two decades since he purposefully stretched *any* muscle.

* * *

Sarah exhaled a deep, happy sigh as she walked from room to room around the Book Nook, admiring the old heartwarming place. She stopped to gaze at the small kid's reading area in the back with Easter books on display, then looked outside at the looming dark gray clouds in the sky.

"Again?" Sarah asked as she peered out the window.

"It's raining all week," Carrie said as she poured a black coffee for a customer.

Sarah bit her lip. "That's weird. I thought it was supposed to end today."

Carrie shook her head. "Nope. It changed. All week now. I mean, it is April showers after all."

Sarah walked behind the counter with Carrie and peeked into the other room after hearing noises. "That guy is back. The one that sleeps on the couch."

Carrie craned her neck to look. "Every day we're open. Without fail, there he is, usually from open to close, though not sleeping the entire time. But man, does he snore loudly."

Sarah stared at the man as he snored with a book on his chest. "Do you think he's homeless? Doesn't he have anything better to do than be here all the time?"

Carrie shrugged. "Beats me."

Sarah's frustration grew. "I don't like that he snores so loudly in a room where other people are trying to read and enjoy their food and drinks. I would like for other people to be able to use that gorgeous velvet couch as well. Does he ever purchase anything?"

Carrie nodded. "Usually a muffin and a chai latte. Once in a while, he'll pay for a newspaper."

Sarah nodded. "I'm going to go talk to him."

Carrie grabbed Sarah's arm before she could move. "Are you sure? Maybe we should leave him be. It might get too awkward."

Sarah slipped out of Carrie's grasp. "Don't worry. I'll be kind," she said as she walked into the room the sleeping man and a few other people sat in.

"Ahem." Sarah cleared her throat loudly as she stood next to him.

The man didn't budge and kept snoring louder than a freight train.

"Excuse me, sir?" Sarah asked as she looked at him.

Another customer sitting nearby in a chair with a book and hot tea chuckled. "Good luck with *that*."

Sarah shifted her eyes, then lightly touched the man. "Excuse me," she said loud enough this time for everyone in the store to turn around.

The older man awoke and abruptly sat up, letting the book on his chest hit the floor. "Oh, guess I fell asleep again."

"Yeah, about that. Your snoring gets quite loud," Sarah said with a light chuckle to break the awkwardness.

The guy laughed. "Really? My wife always told me I snored. I never did believe her. I guess she was right all those times."

Sarah nodded. "I don't mean to pry, but we noticed you're here all the time and that you sleep on this couch a lot …."

The man looked around the room at the other customers, who were now pretending they were doing something else while listening to the conversation. "Yeah, I've probably over-stayed my welcome. You see, my wife passed away a few months ago. I guess it has something to do with that. Well, I'd best be going," he said as he started getting up.

Sarah took a seat on the couch. "Sit. Please. What's your name?"

The man, now feeling embarrassed, cautiously sat down next to Sarah. "It's Ken."

Sarah smiled and held out her hand. "I'm Sarah. I own this place. I didn't want you to leave. I guess I was curious why you're always here and sleeping a lot. Just a little concerned."

Ken took a deep breath. "I think I come here because I'm lonely at home. You spend sixty years with the same person—my wife, Lilly—and when they're gone, you wonder what you will do with yourself. Our only son lives across the country, and it's been hard. Nights especially. I can't sleep. I guess that's why I'm always falling asleep here."

Sarah felt tears welling up in her eyes. "I'm so sorry for the loss of your wife, Ken. I can't imagine how hard that must be for you."

Ken nodded. "Thank you. That's appreciated. I can't tell

you how much joy I get from being here. When the old owners owned the Book Nook, I came in once a week with my wife. We loved visiting and looked forward to picking out which books we'd read that week. This place holds so many happy memories for me."

"You're welcome to stay here as long as you'd like, Ken," Sarah said as she started to get up.

Ken shook his head. "I don't want to bother anyone with my snoring again. How about you just wake me up immediately if it ever happens again."

"I have an idea for the snoring issue," Sarah said as she glanced at the winding stairwell in the back of the room that led to a huge storage area that she'd never done anything with.

Ken touched Sarah's hand. "Thank you for understanding."

"Anytime," Sarah said as she walked back to Carrie at the coffee counter.

"How did it go?" Carrie asked eagerly. "Looks like you talked to him for a while."

"His wife passed recently. He gets his joy—and apparently sleep—from this place. I've got something up my sleeve to solve this snoring problem, though. It involves some work if you want to help," Sarah said as she pulled out a notebook and started drawing a graph.

"I would love to help. By the way, did you ever have that talk with Chris?" Carrie asked.

"Did you overhear that conversation the other day?" Sarah asked.

"Just something about his ex-wife. I wasn't trying to listen in …."

"No. I haven't gotten my thoughts together to discuss it yet. I'm not sure how to go about it. He's asked about it since, but I kind of brushed it off," Sarah said.

Carrie nodded. "I guess I was curious. I've gone through

some things with my husband involving his ex, and it almost ruined us."

Sarah paused as she thought about divulging everything right there, but she couldn't find the words. She hated putting any energy into the strange situation, and she surely didn't want it to ruin the wonderful thing she had going with Chris. Then again, was there something she didn't know about him? Was Roberta's warning truthful?

CHAPTER NINE

After school the next day, Liz and Margaret worked on setting up an Easter egg dying station on the dining room table for the kids.

Margaret laid down a plastic tablecloth, while Liz put out the different colored dye cups with spoons.

"Oh, we can't forget the hard-boiled eggs," Margaret said as she walked into her kitchen and grabbed a few dozen eggs in cartons and carefully placed them on the table.

"OK, kids. Come in here and dye Easter eggs," Liz yelled up the steps.

Minutes later, Harper and Abby rushed down the steps while Michael and Steven walked in from the living room where they'd been playing games on their phones.

Michael rolled his eyes. "Mom, I think we're getting too old for this."

Steven shrugged as he picked up an egg and plopped it into a cup with red dye. "There, I dyed an egg."

Liz chuckled. "Just have some fun with it. Be creative. Aunt Margaret and I are much older than you two, and we want to dye eggs, don't we, Margaret?"

Margaret nodded as she took a seat next to Harper. "That's right. Never too old for this kind of fun."

Abby reached over for some sparkles to put on her egg, while Harper attempted to draw a unicorn on hers.

Liz placed some Easter Bunny stickers on her egg before she noticed Michael sitting looking at his phone, half paying attention to the egg he was dipping in a cup of dye. "You OK over there?"

Michael feverishly texted someone. "It's Hailey. She just asked if we're going to the spring dance tomorrow."

Liz glanced at Margaret, then back at Michael. "Well, your dad and I are chaperoning the dance, so I certainly hope you are."

Michael smiled at his phone. "If Hailey is going, I'll be there."

Steven chuckled. "He's got a thing for her."

Michael turned tomato red, then stared at Steven. "And you like Jamie."

Steven rolled his eyes. "So what. Maybe I do. At least I admit it."

Liz cleared her throat. "So, they're your girlfriends? I thought you were all just friends."

Margaret tried to hide her laughter as she decorated her eggs. The conversation was getting more awkward by the minute.

Michael shrugged. "I guess?"

Steven cut in. "Don't sugarcoat it. I saw you and Hailey kiss the other day outside."

Liz's eyes widened, not sure of what to say to that.

Michael sighed. "And you kissed Jamie."

Harper and Abby started laughing. "K-I-S-S-I-N-G," they both said aloud together.

Margaret cleared her throat. "So, are you all going to the dance together?" she asked the boys.

Michael shook his head. "They asked us to meet them there."

"Oh," Liz said, wondering why that was the case.

"Can we get off this topic?" Steven said as he reached over Abby for the markers.

Liz nodded. "Surely. We'll talk about something else. Margaret, have you heard back from any other B&Bs about their availability for the five rooms for Maxine?"

Margaret nodded. "I heard back from two more this morning. They're booked solid. I never realized how many people come to Cape May on Easter."

Liz shook her head and sighed. "I called a few places this morning. Nothing. What about Hugh and Betty at Morning Dew Cottage next door? Did you hear back from them yet?"

Margaret sighed. "They finally got back to me. They're visiting family in Arizona. The place is closed up until next week."

"OK, we're done!" Harper said as her and Abby got up and pushed their chairs back under the table. "Can we go watch TV?"

Margaret looked at their finished eggs, surprised they were done so fast. "That's fine. Stay close."

Michael and Steven took that as their cue to get up and follow the girls while texting on their phones.

Liz stared at the mess on the table, then looked at Margaret and laughed. "Guess we should clean up now."

Margaret shook her head. "I'm not finished. Sit here and decorate eggs with me. We can chat."

Moments later, there was a knock at the door.

"Who's that?" Margaret asked.

Liz smacked her forehead. "I forgot to tell you, I invited Donna and Sarah over."

Margaret jumped up. "Perfect. I need to lower my stress over this B&B debacle. You get the door, and I'll get the wine, cheese, and crackers."

Minutes later, they were all sitting at the table dying Easters eggs and enjoying a glass of sauvignon blanc.

Donna took a sip from her wineglass. "You know, Dale is having a terrible time at the restaurant lately."

"Really?" Liz asked.

Donna nodded. "Yes, he's getting much busier than he or his staff can handle. He's got to put some new systems in place. The poor guy always comes home looking so stressed."

"Sorry to hear that, but that's great he's getting so much business. I'm sure he'll figure it out in no time," Margaret said.

Donna nodded. "I sure hope so. He installed a few more cameras in the restaurant yesterday. He thinks someone is stealing from the cash drawer."

Liz shook her head. "That's awful. Thankfully, Greg has never dealt with that."

"It is. I'm hoping he gets some answers soon. He doesn't deserve this. He's nothing but patient and kind with his staff, and he pays them well," Donna said, getting emotional.

Sarah popped a piece of cheese in her mouth. "Well, hopefully, those cameras can give him answers."

Margaret glanced into the living room at the kids watching television, then back at Sarah. "So, the Book Nook is working out nicely?"

Sarah smiled widely. "It is. I'm in love with the place. Business is great, and I love being closed on Mondays and Tuesdays. I have so much more time for myself lately. Speaking of which, I was going to bring Sam today, but Roberta had other plans for him," she said as she glanced at Donna's engagement ring. "Can I see your ring?" Sarah asked as she took Donna's hand.

Donna became uneasy as Sarah studied it. "I could have sworn this was the ring Chris initially had in his hand when he went to propose. Are you sure it wasn't?" Sarah asked.

Margaret and Liz's eyes widened as they took big gulps of their wine.

Donna finished her wine, then set her glass down and stared Sarah in the eyes. "Fine. You really want to know what happened? I swore to Dale, I would not tell."

Sarah nodded.

Donna looked at her ring, twisting it on her finger. "This is Dale's grandmother's ring. This was meant to be mine. Dale lost it in the ocean when he went out to save a boy from drowning. Chris was helping him look for it. Dale had already bought another ring for me, thinking they'd never find it. The night that Chris proposed, he accidentally had this ring, Dale's family heirloom, so they switched on the fly. That ring on your finger is what Dale bought as a backup."

Sarah's eyes widened as she stared at her hand. "So, Chris didn't pick out my ring? It's Dale's ring?"

Donna nodded. "Yes."

Tears welled in Sarah eyes. "Did Chris even *want* to propose?"

Donna put her arm around Sarah. "Yes, I'm sure he did. It was all just a big mix-up. Now, do you see why I haven't said anything since? I didn't want to ruin that moment you two had because that's what matters the most here. I didn't want to be the one that messed up your engagement."

Sarah shook her head. "I can't marry him. I can't. Until I get the whole truth from him. Between running into his ex-wife and her telling me to basically run, and now this ...farce?"

Margaret put her hand on Sarah's. "Just talk to him. I'm sure there's an explanation."

"He's away on a two-night fishing trip, but as soon as he gets back on Saturday, I'm getting answers," Sarah said as she took another bite of cheese.

* * *

That evening, Dale worked the manager shift for their Thursday dinner rush at Donna's Restaurant. The place had closed, and aside from Carlos, the cook, he was the only one there in the empty restaurant.

"I'll see you later, Dale," Carlos said as he pulled off his apron, folded it up, and put his jacket on.

Dale stopped counting the money in the drawer and looked up. "Take care, Carlos. I guess I'll be seeing you next week?"

Carlos nodded. "Yep. I finally have off for a holiday. That's unheard of in the restaurant industry. I can't remember the last time I had Easter off."

Dale smiled. "Well, I'm glad you'll be able to rest and enjoy it. I considered staying open on Easter, but I thought we all needed a break and some time with our family, especially with how crazy things have been."

Carlos chuckled. "You're telling me. It's like we got a whole new staff this spring and had to start from scratch."

"Well, changes are coming. Trust me. It will get better, and hopefully, we won't have to deal with this again in the future. See you later, Carlos," Dale said as he went back to counting the money drawer again.

Carlos left, and the restaurant got eerily quiet. The lights were still dimmed from when the dinner crowd was there, and the only thing that could be heard was the humming of the refrigerator in the kitchen.

Dale finished counting the drawer and sat up on the barstool. "The money's all there. That's the first time that's happened in a while. Huh."

As Dale thought for a moment, a knock came at the front door. Dale walked over and smiled as he let Donna inside.

"Hey. Whatcha doing?" Dale asked as he hugged and kissed Donna.

Donna took a deep breath. "I just left Margaret's house. I've been there for hours talking with the girls. I thought I'd stop by on the way home and see if you were still here."

Dale went and sat on the stool at the bar again, and Donna pulled up a seat next to him. "It's weird. I just counted the money drawer, and for the first time in weeks, there isn't any money missing."

Donna bit her lip. "Interesting. Why do you think that is?"

Dale shrugged. "I don't know."

Donna thought for a moment. "Didn't you work both lunch and dinner shifts today for the first time since last year?"

Dale nodded. "Yes, what are you getting at?"

Donna sat straight up. "Did you check the new cameras you put in yesterday?"

Dale's eyes widened as he pulled out his phone. "That's right. I forgot about that. I have remote access from my phone. I think it starts me at yesterday morning after I turned them on."

Donna peered over his shoulder as they watched. "This is going to be hours. We don't have time for that. Fast-forward until you see someone at the money drawer."

After thirty minutes of fast-forwarding and stopping and fast-forwarding, something grabbed Donna's eye. "Wait. Rewind it. There."

Dale rewound the footage to the darkened bar area without any customers in view. "This must be after we closed last night."

Donna stared at the screen. "Look. Who's that?"

Dale widened his eyes. "That's Frank, one of my managers."

Donna shook her head. "And there it is. He just looked around the room and pocketed money from the drawer."

Dale replayed the footage. "You're right. The days money is missing always seem to be when he's working, and now I have proof."

Donna sighed. "Well, it looks like you're going to have to resolve that issue quickly."

Dale nodded. "Yes, I will, and I'm not granting access to the money drawer to servers anymore. They're going to have to ask the bartenders to make change for them. The less people in there, the better. I just finished telling Carlos about how I'm implanting changes, and this will be added to the top of the list."

Donna stared at her feet, starting to feel a little nervous.

"What? What are you thinking about?" Dale asked.

Donna fumbled with her words. "Now might be a bad time to tell you this …."

Dale's eyes widened. "What? Is the kitchen OK?"

Donna shook her head. "The kitchen is fine. The house is fine."

"Then what?" Dale asked, anxiety creeping in.

"I kind of told Sarah about what happened with the rings," Donna said.

Dale rubbed his hand over his face. "Well, I guess Chris hates me now."

Donna put her hand on Dale's shoulder. "Look, she saw what happened. She saw the ring that's on my hand in the ring box, and then she saw you two exchange rings. She knew something fishy happened, and I couldn't keep it from her when she asked. She needed to know. Chris can't be mad at you, she saw it happen. He needs to be honest with her anyway."

Dale stood up and stretched his arms. "Well, I sure hope this doesn't cause any serious issues with them. I would feel terrible."

"I hope so too," Donna said as she stood up next to Dale.

Dale put his arms around Donna and leaned his head on her shoulder. "I'm exhausted. Remind me to never open a new restaurant again. I can't wait until things get better here."

Donna made a sad face. "I'm always here to help if you need it. What's going to happen with Frank?"

Dale sighed deeply. "I'm giving him a call tonight. He's due in tomorrow, and I can't have someone here that's been stealing."

Donna widened her eyes. "That's going to be awkward."

Dale shook his head. "You're telling me. I've never dealt with this kind of situation before. I'm not even sure how to go about confronting him."

Donna pointed to Dale's phone. "Tell him you have security footage showing him pocketing money out of the drawer. It says it's after dinner hours, so it's not like he was making change."

Suddenly, a knock came at the door, and Donna and Dale both looked over to see Greg waving at them.

Dale walked over to let Greg in.

"Hey, guys. Saw you two through the window as I was leaving for the night. Tonight was insanely busy at Heirloom," Greg said as he looked around the room.

Dale nodded. "It was crazy here, too, but you know what's really crazy? I figured out my manager, Frank, is the one who has been stealing from the money drawer."

"You're kidding," Greg said, dumbfounded.

Dale folded his arms. "I'm going to call him pretty soon to fire him. It's a shame because I like him."

Greg sighed. "Man, I'm so sorry. Running a business isn't easy."

Dale waved his hand. "It is what it is. Speaking of business, did you end up getting more reservations for Easter brunch?"

Greg shook his head. "Nope. It's my own fault, but the good part is I decided to cancel the brunch and give my staff the day off for Easter. They're elated."

Dale smiled. "Same here. I think we made a good choice."

CHAPTER TEN

Margaret stood on the Seahorse Inn's large wraparound porch watching the rain fall on the street, and feeling more stressed than ever.

Dolly opened the front door and peeked out. "Our Easter guests should be arriving any moment."

"I know. I don't know what I'm going to do with Maxine's family," Margaret said as she slumped into the swinging chair to rock back and forth.

Dolly nodded, then caught a glimpse of a car pulling into the driveway of the Morning Dew Cottage next door. "Is that Betty and Hugh? I thought they were visiting family across the country?"

Margaret stood up. "They were supposed to be," she said as she walked out into the rain and watched them pull their suitcases out of the car and run up the steps of their B&B before walking inside.

Dolly shifted her eyes. "Margaret, you're standing in the pouring rain. What are you doing?"

Margaret looked up at Dolly. "I'll be right back," she said as she ran towards the Morning Dew Cottage.

After walking up the stairs to the B&B, Margaret knocked on the door.

"Margaret. You're soaked!" Betty exclaimed when she answered the door. "Get inside."

Hugh walked into the kitchen, opened a drawer, and pulled out a dish towel before tossing it to Margaret.

"I thought you guys were away this weekend?" Margaret asked as she toweled her face off.

Hugh shook his head. "Our flight got delayed, then canceled. The next flight wasn't until after Easter."

Betty cut in. "Then, we come to find out, a lot of the family had come down with a stomach bug. So, we're rescheduling for another time. Unfortunately, it didn't work out. Is everything OK, Margaret?"

Margaret shook her head. "I need a favor from you two, and I hate to do this right after you went through all of that, but we're in over our heads next door at the Seahorse Inn."

Betty turned on the dining room lights and sat down. "Come, sit. Tell us what's going on," she said as Hugh took a seat next to her.

Margaret sat down and took a deep breath. "We need five rooms for our B&B guests who are arriving in fifteen minutes. Liz overbooked us, and I told the family with the five rooms that I'd find them other accommodations. Well, as it turns out, nobody has any openings. None. Nada. Zilch. If I can't find somewhere for them to stay, our last resort is putting them up in our homes."

Hugh laughed. Then, Betty looked at Hugh and started laughing herself. And they couldn't stop.

Margaret's eyes widened. "What's so funny?"

Betty put her hand on Margaret's. "We're not laughing at you, dear. We're laughing because this exact thing happened to us many years ago … and guess who ended up helping us out?"

Margaret shrugged. "My great-aunt and uncle?"

Hugh smiled. "Yep, back when we were good friends. They got us out of that pickle."

Margaret paused, waiting to see what they would say next.

"We'll definitely help you out. In fact, we would be glad to. We have eight guest rooms, and we'd be glad to take in that family that needs five," Betty said as she wiped the tears of laughter from her eyes.

Margaret jumped up and hugged Betty and Hugh. "I can't even tell you how happy and relieved I am to hear this right now. They're literally going to be here any minute."

Hugh nodded. "Well, it works out nicely, that's for sure."

Margaret looked towards the kitchen. "Well, I told them they could still come over for Easter brunch and our weekend activities. Is that OK?"

Betty smiled. "Perfectly fine. We'll work together to make it a great Easter weekend for everyone."

Margaret hugged Betty again. "I have a feeling we're going to all enjoy this holiday weekend. I'll be over shortly to escort the guests in. Then, we'll talk soon. Thanks again," Margaret said as she headed back outside into the rain.

Hugh put his arm around Betty and looked at her. "I guess it was good that we cleaned the rooms immediately after our last guests left."

Betty chuckled. "And washed all the linens. I mean, we could have waited for our house cleaners to come, but you were insistent on getting it done before we left."

Hugh looked around the spotless B&B. "Well, you know I like to tidy up *everything* before we go on vacation. I prefer to come home to a clean house. It helps me relax when we go away."

Betty nodded. "Oh, I totally agree, and now it's worked out to help Margaret and Liz."

A knock came at the door, and there stood Margaret with the large family and their luggage on the Morning Dew's front porch out of the rain.

Betty opened the door wide. "Come in. Come in. Welcome to The Morning Dew Cottage."

Hugh stood behind her smiling as they all walked in, with Margaret coming in last.

Betty walked the new guests to their rooms, while Margaret hung back with Hugh. "You guys are lifesavers. Let me know if there's anything you need over here," Margaret said as she opened the front door and stepped back onto the porch.

Hugh chuckled. "We'll be fine. This isn't our first rodeo, after all."

* * *

Across town at the Book Nook, Sarah stood at the top of the winding staircase in the storage room and looked down the stairs.

"*Psst*. Carrie." Sarah tried to whisper loudly so as to not disturb any of the customers.

Carrie walked to the bottom of the stairs. "What's up? Are you finished up there?"

Sarah nodded joyfully. "I think so. Is Ken down there anywhere?"

Carrie pointed behind her. "He's in the front looking at the *Just In* book display. Do you want me to get him?"

"Yes, please. Show him the way up. I can't wait for him to see this," Sarah said as she walked away from the stairs.

Carrie brought Ken up the stairs and stood with him as he looked at the old storage room that had been converted into a gorgeous sitting area, complete with another velvet couch.

Sarah opened her arms wide. "Ken, what do you think?"

Ken's eyes glistened as they looked around the room at the old paintings hanging on the walls and the shelves of books and stained-glass lamps on the tables next to the chairs. "This is something."

Sarah nodded, feeling proud of herself. "You inspired me

to clean up this space. Can you believe I bought this couch three months ago and never found any room for it downstairs? It's been sitting up here with boxes all over it. These paintings on the wall had been collecting dust on the ground. I even had this area rug, and it makes it so cozy up here."

Ken flopped onto the couch and kicked his feet up on the ottoman, watching all of the dancing colored lights from the small stained-glass windows hit different areas of the room. "I absolutely love it. You did this for me?"

Sarah put her arm around Carrie's shoulders. "We did it for you. Now you can have your own space and stay as long as you want. I know grief can be hard, but we want to see you happy."

Ken felt tears welling up in his eyes. "No one has ever done something like this for me. I … don't know what to say."

Carrie cut in. "You can start by telling me what kind of coffee you want. I'll bring you some."

Ken smiled. "You know me. I'll take a chai latte and a blueberry muffin, of course."

* * *

By lunchtime, the Seahorse guests had all been checked in, and Dolly, Kim, Bonnie, Irene, and Jackie were holding down the fort while Margaret and Liz got some last-minute Easter basket shopping done for the kids and the Easter egg hunt.

They ended up at The Original Fudge Kitchen in the Washington Street Mall, looking at all of the chocolates and candy.

Liz picked up a stack of hollow chocolate Easter bunnies and put them in her basket as Margaret studied some coconut cream stuffed chocolate eggs, trying to decide if the girls would like them.

Liz bit her lip. "I'd go with the peanut butter eggs if I were you."

Margaret nodded. "You're right. They don't like coconut."

Liz laughed. "You're the one that loves coconut. Buy it for yourself."

Margaret waved Liz off. "Nah. I'm not shopping for me," she said as she looked at bags of jelly beans. "What should we buy to put inside the eggs for the egg hunt on the beach?"

Liz grabbed the jelly beans and put them in her basket. "I'm thinking individually wrapped candies and chocolates and maybe stickers, little toys, and erasers? Mix it up, you know?"

"Good idea," Margaret said as she spotted some chocolate covered pretzels in the glass case for Dave.

Liz set her basket on the counter and pulled out her wallet as an employee rang her up. She looked over at Margaret who was still looking in the glass case. "I'm amazed how everything worked out with the overbooked guests. I can't thank you enough for figuring out how to fix my mistake."

Margaret smiled at Liz. "Well, Betty and Hugh laughed when I told them what happened. They said the same thing happened to them years ago. Great-Aunt Mary and Uncle Lou helped them out. So, you're not alone. It happens, and usually your friends are there to help."

Liz sighed. "Well, now we owe them one. Seriously."

"Oh, I know," Margaret said with a chuckle.

* * *

After dinner, Bob was walking the Wildwood Boardwalk after getting in a good ten minutes of upper and lower body stretching beforehand. As he powered over the wooden boards, he caught glimpses of scattered shops getting ready to open for the season. Some pizza places with their bright lights were already doing business, but the piers with roller coasters sat empty and silent. Bob looked at his pedometer on his phone as a cool breeze came through. He had already gotten in two and half miles, so he decided to turn back towards his car that was near the convention center. At first, he walked, but then he decided to try and give jogging a try again.

As he jogged towards the convention center, someone ran by, then stopped.

"Bob?"

Bob slowed to a walk, and noticed it was Tim, who was out jogging too. "Tim. Funny seeing you here."

Tim chuckled. "I thought you said you didn't jog?"

Bob shook his head and laughed. "It just kind of happened. I finally realized that I needed to start stretching. My legs were cramping up horribly."

Tim nodded. "Oh yes, that's a must. Well, I'm proud of you. That didn't take much time at all."

Bob shrugged. "I'm as surprised as you. Well, if you don't mind jogging slow, I'd like to join you for a run sometime. Give me a few weeks to get into my groove."

Tim smiled and put his hand on Bob's shoulder. "This is great to hear. I actually have a running group that I jog with, if you're ever interested. We do the Broad Street Run in Philadelphia, and a bunch of other stuff."

Bob's eyes widened. "I don't know about that."

Tim chuckled. "Well, it's always on the table if you want to think about it."

They shook hands, said their goodbyes, and Bob was back in his car, wondering what other surprises his future would hold. He felt good, really good. Maybe it was never too late to start working on fitness after all.

Just as he was about to reverse the car out of the parking space, his phone rang.

"Judy. I'm on my way home. I'll be there in about ten minutes or so."

Judy nodded. "Good, because I need help bringing all this junk out of the basement and into the living room. We're having a yard sale tomorrow."

Bob's eyes widened. "What? Who is?"

Judy cleared her throat. "I just found out there's a neighborhood-wide yard sale tomorrow. We can get rid of all the stuff taking up room in those storage bins from our old house. It'll give us more space in the basement."

Bob took a deep breath. "You've got a full house of people coming the next day for Easter. Do you really think we'll have time to do this?"

Judy waved her hand in the air. "I can do all my prep tomorrow evening, and you can set up the rest of the tables and chairs then too. The yard sale is from eight to noon. What do you say?"

Bob paused a moment. "Well, if it's what you want to do …. What kind of things do we have to sell anyway?"

Judy looked around in a dusty bin. "Looks like I've got a lot of baskets and odds and ends. A set of glasses, dishes … you know that kind of stuff."

"Well, I guess we'll make it work. I'll see you when I get home," Bob said as he put the car in reverse.

* * *

That evening, Greg and Liz stood in the high school's decorated gymnasium. Liz wore a black dress and heels while Greg opted for khakis and a tucked-in plaid button-down shirt. Different colored lights flashed around the room as the DJ played upbeat music.

"OK, everyone. Let's get ready to dance!" the DJ said as he put on a new song.

Liz and Greg stood off to the side, casually watching the students mill about the gymnasium, finding their friends and then picking a corner to stand in and talk.

"Nobody is dancing," Liz said as she scanned the room.

Greg shrugged as he picked up a carrot stick from the food table and dunked it into some French onion dip. "I think that might be relatively normal for this age. They all feel too awkward."

Liz thought for a moment. "I feel like Margaret and I and all of our friends and boyfriends would dance all night at these things. My how things have changed."

Greg laughed. "That was probably not your freshman year of high school, but who knows."

"Have you seen Michael or Steven?" Liz asked as she watched a group of boys walk in together.

Greg shook his head. "Other than when we dropped them off at the front door before parking, no."

Liz shifted her eyes. "Where would they be? I mean, the only reason I'm doing this is because it's *their* dance for Pete's sake."

Greg looked around the gym, his eyes landing on a group of girls to the side. "Well, there's Hailey and Jamie."

Liz glanced in their direction. "Huh."

"Oh, I think I found the boys," Greg said, motioning to the top of the bleachers that weren't pulled out where Michael, Steven, and six other boys were sitting.

Liz's eyes widened. "What? How did they get up there?"

Greg walked towards them and motioned for them to come down. "Boys, you're not supposed to be up there. There's a reason these bleachers aren't pulled out. They don't want anyone sitting on them."

Michael and Steven rolled their eyes, jumped down, then found a corner of the room with the rest of their friends to stand in far away from their *embarrassing* parents.

The song ended and the DJ got back on the microphone. "OK, everyone, we're going to slow things down a little," he said as he played a slow love song.

The mood in the room changed immediately as every boy looked at the girl they wanted to dance with. Michael and Steven both walked towards Hailey and Jamie but were intercepted by two other boys.

Michael and Steven felt their hearts drop as they watched the girls that they both had crushes on slow dance with other boys.

Liz looked at Greg. "Did you see that? This isn't good."

Greg stared straight at the boys, knowing full well how they were feeling in that moment. "No, it's not. I've been there."

Liz nudged Greg. "Greg, Michael and Steven are walking towards us. Act calm. Pretend you didn't see anything."

Moments later, Michael and Steven stood before them, looking miserable. "We'd like to go home now, please," Steven said.

Liz glanced at Greg. "Well, we can't leave until the dance is over. We signed up to be chaperones. There's only another hour left. Go hang out with your friends. Enjoy yourselves."

Michael scoffed. "We really don't want to be here right now ... friends or not."

Just then, the DJ switched the song back to an upbeat dance song and almost all of the students flooded the floor, dancing and getting down.

Greg looked up to see Michael and Steven's group of guy friends approaching. "Look, they're all coming over to get you two."

Michael and Steven turned around to face their friends, who immediately put their arms around their shoulders and walked them to the dance floor, where they all started doing the funniest dance moves Liz and Greg had ever seen. The boys were now all laughing at each other and enjoying themselves.

Liz grinned. "Well, that turned around quickly."

Greg nodded. "It pays to have good friends. That's for sure."

CHAPTER ELEVEN

Judy and Bob busily added price tags to their yard sale items displayed on their tables the next morning.

Bob picked up a half-used bottle of lotion. "Judy, what is *this* doing here? Nobody will want this."

Judy shrugged. "Well, it can't hurt putting it out. I no longer want it."

Bob shook his head and chuckled as he looked at the clothing rack off to the side stuffed with Judy's clothing, spotting items Judy may have had when they first met.

Their neighbor, Angela, walked up holding two hot coffees in paper cups. "Thought I'd bring you two some fresh caffeine," she said handing them over.

"Oh, you're too kind. Thank you," Judy said as she blew on the coffee and took a sip. "This is our first time doing the neighborhood yard sale. What should we expect?" Judy asked.

Angela smiled and waved to another person crossing the street, then sighed. "Oh, a lot of people look forward to this event. There should be a pretty good turnout. We've got most of the neighbors on this street doing it this year too," she said as she looked at all the yard sale setups down the block.

Bob took a sip of his coffee as he looked at the huge

stack of vintage board games laid out on a blanket next to him. "Well, I sure hope they like old stuff. We've got a lot of it."

Angela nodded. "I'm sure you'll do just fine. Come get us if you need any help," she said as she headed back across the street to her house.

Judy picked up a half-used bottle of perfume from the '90s with a fifty-cent price sticker slapped on it, and spritzed herself.

Bob stared at her.

"What?" Judy asked. "You said nobody would want it anyway. Might as well get a last use out of it."

Judy quickly put the perfume back on the table as she saw some people approaching. "Bob, our first customers," she whispered excitedly.

Bob chuckled. "Let's just call them browsers. They aren't a customer until they buy something."

The people rummaged through the items, then abruptly left, heading to the neighbor's setup.

Judy's heart sank. "Well, I don't think anyone wants our old stuff, Bob. Maybe this was a waste of time?"

Bob opened two vintage folding lawn chairs and set them up behind the table. "Here. Sit. Let's just enjoy being out here. Maybe we'll sell a couple things in the process."

Judy rolled her eyes, feeling frustrated, and pulled an old romance book out of the large stack of books on the table. She opened it and started reading.

Ten minutes later, a large crowd of people had descended onto their items for sale.

A college-aged girl's eyes widened as she looked through the clothing rack, pulling one thing after another into her arms. "Oh my gosh, I've hit the jackpot!" she exclaimed as she held up a pristine 1960s green floral dress.

Judy looked up from her book and smiled. "That was mine way back when. Isn't it great?"

The girl held the dress up to her body, getting an idea for

the fit. It seemed to be the perfect match. "It's wonderful. I'll take everything on this rack."

Judy stood up and clapped her hands excitedly. "Well, they're five dollars each, but I'll give you everything for fifty. How's that?"

"Perfect," the girl said as she got out her wallet.

Bob watched as someone approached him with a box. "How much for all these comic books, sir?"

Bob's eyes widened. "My comic books? How did they get in there? Oh, I'm sorry. There's been a mistake. They're not for sale."

"I'll give you a hundred bucks for the entire box," the guy said.

Bob was taken aback. "I'm sorry. I can't part with them, even for a hundred dollars."

The guy looked disappointed and put the box down on the table and left.

Judy shrugged. "I may have brought that box out not knowing what was in there."

Bob took the box back inside, then scoured the rest of the items for sale, making sure nothing else of importance was out there.

Moments later, Margaret and Dave arrived with the girls.

"Hi, Mom and Dad," Margaret said as she glanced at some items on the table. "How's the yard sale going?"

Judy smiled. "It's going pretty good so far. Where are you all off to?"

Dave picked up a bag of old potpourri, looked at it, then put it down "Headed to the Doo Dah Parade in Ocean City. Margaret has always wanted to go."

"Oh, that will be fun. When does it start?" Bob asked.

"Noon," Margaret said as some items on a blanket caught her eye. She walked over and bent down to rummage through them. "My childhood toys from the eighties! I've been looking for these for years. Why didn't you tell me that you found them?"

Judy shrugged. "I guess I forgot. I didn't think you'd want some old Strawberry Shortcake dolls and what not."

Margaret quickly scooped up all the toys and threw them into a box. "Sorry, but I'm taking these. I've always wanted to introduce my beloved vintage toys to the girls, and I might as well do it now before they're too old for them."

Bob nodded. "That's fine, dear. They're yours."

Margaret opened her car's truck and stuffed the big box in, then turned around to find Dave, Harper, and Abby sitting on the grass going through the board game stacks.

Harper looked up, noticing Margaret was watching. "Mom, we want this old Candy Land game."

Abby stood up, holding another game. "And this Parcheesi one."

"Well, we might as well throw this one in the car too," Dave said with a chuckle as he held up Battleship.

Margaret reached into her purse, pulling out a twenty-dollar bill and handed it to Judy. "Here, Mom. This is for the games. Keep the extra."

Judy scoffed. "You can have the games for free, hon. They were probably yours and Liz's games anyway."

Margaret rolled her eyes. "Just take it. Use it towards Easter dinner. By the way, is it OK if I invite Betty and Hugh from the Morning Dew Cottage over tomorrow? They've been life-savers with helping us this holiday weekend with an overbooking. They were supposed to be with family this weekend, so I thought it'd be nice to invite them over."

Bob's eyes widened as he looked at Judy. "I think we're going to have to rent out a neighbor's house *and* the VFW at this point."

Judy waved Bob off. "I would love for them to come."

Margaret threw her arms around Judy's shoulders. "Perfect, thank you. Well, we'd better head out. I want to get breakfast at Uncle Bill's in Ocean City before the parade. I'll call you later."

Judy nodded as her phone rang. She noticed it was Linda. "OK, we'll talk later today. You all have fun." She picked up her phone as Margaret, Dave, and the girls loaded into the car and left.

"Good morning, Linda," Judy said as another large crowd approached their yard.

Linda nodded. "Good morning, sister. Really quick, as I'm about to ring up my items at the grocery store. Can I bring Rose and Dick tomorrow, you know, my in-laws? Mike just got word that they're going to be in town. For some reason, they forgot we weren't hosting Easter this year."

Judy laughed as she watched Bob take some money from customers. "Well, we're going to have a full house, basement, and yard. That's for sure. Bring 'em. You know I love a big gathering."

Linda gave a huge sigh of relief. "So glad to hear this. Thank you, Judy."

"I forgot to tell you. I talked to Carol."

Linda laughed. "So did I. We both apologized. I guess I had left some things out from what I told you, huh?"

Judy nodded. "Yes, you did. You forgot to mention how you accidentally stood her up a few times before. Keep your phone on, would you?"

Linda rolled her eyes playfully. "I'll try. Carol already bought me a wall calendar."

* * *

By noon, the Doo Dah Parade was getting underway, and Margaret, Dave, and the girls had secured their viewing spot on the Ocean City Boardwalk.

Margaret smiled when she heard horns and drums getting louder as a marching band approached. The girls clapped along as the marching band played by them before noticing someone casually walking by.

"Is that Dad again?" Harper asked as she squinted her eyes.

Margaret looked at Dave, then glanced over to see her ex-husband walking through the crowd, coming towards them. "It is."

Paul was about to walk by them when Abby screeched, "Dad!"

Paul abruptly turned around, having not noticed them. "Oh my goodness. So funny seeing you two here," he said as he gave Abby a hug, while putting his arm around Harper.

Dave stuck his hand out, and Paul shook it, while nodding at Margaret.

"What's up, Paul? You here for the parade?"

Paul gave a nervous laugh. "Actually, no. I had no idea this parade was even happening. I'm actually trying to get back to my car. It's quite an obstacle course out here."

Margaret chuckled. "Well, you can stay here and watch the parade if you want. We've got some room."

Paul hesitated, then Harper cut in. "Where's Katie?"

Paul looked at his feet, then back up at Margaret and Dave. "We're not together anymore."

Everyone's eyes widened, including Harper's and Abby's.

"It is what it is," Paul said as he looked around at the crowd, trying to veer away from the subject.

Abby tugged on Paul's sleeve. "Are we still going to have a baby sibling?"

Paul kneeled down to look Abby and Harper in the eyes. "As it turns out, no. I'm sorry."

Margaret glanced at Dave, not knowing whether she was more shocked that he was having a baby or that he wasn't.

"What's going on, Paul?" Margaret asked, confusion setting in.

Paul sighed and pulled Dave and Margaret aside. "She

came out and told me that it wasn't my baby. She had been seeing someone else while we were together, and after doing some math, realized it couldn't have been mine. I actually just found out about this right before I ran into you guys. It's been pretty soul crushing, actually."

Dave put his hand on Paul's shoulder to console him, while Margaret thought for a moment. Paul was finally getting a taste of his own medicine after he had cheated on Margaret with Sandy. That time he left that note on the counter telling her he was leaving. All the emails she found between them, when she never knew what was going on.

Paul looked at Margaret who was staring off into the distance. "I know what you're thinking."

Margaret snapped out of her daze. "You probably do, but it doesn't mean I don't sympathize with you. It's awful what happened, especially since you thought you were having another baby."

Dave put his arm around Margaret's waist, which made her feel so supported and loved in that moment. It was hard for her to harbor bad feelings for Paul, when ending that marriage brought her the best man she could have imagined —Dave.

Paul nodded. "It's crazy. Can you imagine me having another baby? At this age?"

Margaret shrugged. "I mean, it happens, but I'll admit when the girls told me, I started to wonder how it would affect them."

Paul sighed. "The girls would never take a back seat to anyone else, if that's what you were wondering."

Just then, Dale and Donna pushed through the crowd, waving wildly at Margaret and Dave.

"Hi, guys! You didn't tell me you were coming," Margaret said as she hugged them.

Paul stood awkwardly looking at Dave. "Well, I'm going to say goodbye to the girls and head out. It's been a day."

Dave smiled and gave Paul a back-pat hug. "Take care, man. You'll be fine."

Dale stood next to Dave as Donna and Margaret caught up while watching the parade. "Good to see you, man. Everything going well?"

Dave nodded, while turning his backwards hat forward to block the sun. "It's going. How about you? I hear the restaurant has been a bit stressful."

Dale sighed. "It hasn't been easy. I had to fire an employee —one of my managers that was stealing—and things were running amok for a bit. I've started holding mandatory meetings with my employees before lunch and dinner shifts, and the restaurant already seems to be running better. My manager, Dixie, is helping me get everything under control, and I'm excited for what's to come.

Dave smiled. "That's great. I'm sorry to hear about your manager stealing, though. Any suitors lined up?"

Dale nodded. "Actually, yes. Dixie recommended someone she used to work with that's now looking to relocate in Cape May. I'm meeting with them tomorrow."

"Well, I'll cross my fingers for you," Dave said as Pitman's Original Hobo Band, dressed in patched-up funny clothing, loudly marched by playing their instruments.

Meanwhile on the other end of the boardwalk, Chris and Sarah walked towards the parade.

Chris glanced at Sarah as they walked. "You're being quiet."

Sarah shrugged. "I've had a lot on my mind."

Chris shifted his eyes. "What? With work?"

Sarah shrugged again. "Not really."

Chris stopped walking and took Sarah's hand in his. "What's wrong?"

Sarah looked down the boardwalk, then back at Chris. "I know about the ring."

Chris paused for a moment, took a deep breath, then

stared towards the parade before looking at Sarah. "So, you know. You know that the ring I gave you was Dale's ring meant for Donna."

Sarah pursed her lips. "Yes. Do you even want to get married? Is this all a lie?"

Chris nodded. "Yes, I wanted to get married. Did I plan to propose to you that night? No. It just happened, but it felt right, so I went with it."

Sarah laughed sarcastically. "You *went* with it? You don't just *go with it* when it comes to engagements. Those are planned. It's a major life decision."

Chris ran his fingers through his hair, feeling frustration set in. "Look, I want to marry you. I already had a ring for you before I proposed. It's still at the house. I didn't know what to do with it, and I was afraid for you to find out about the ring being Dale's."

Sarah was shocked. "You had a ring for me already? Are you serious?"

Chris sighed. "Yes, I'd bought it the day before. I ended up paying Dale for his new ring after I accidentally proposed to you with it."

"Can I see the ring?" Sarah asked.

"We can set that up" Chris said with a smile.

Sarah stared out at the ocean. "There is one more thing."

Chris's eyes widened, afraid of what else was about to be divulged.

"When I ran into Roberta, she basically tried warning me about you. She told me that you said marriage ruined you two, but she suspected you were cheating. That you were always taking phone calls at night outside and staying late at the docks. It was weird …."

Chris laughed. "Oh, I did take phone calls at night outside, and I did stay very late at the docks. That part is true, but it wasn't because I was cheating. It was for my own sanity. Those phone calls? Those were with my friends. I needed someone to vent to. Those late nights at the docks? I was happier there than I was at home."

Sarah's eyes widened. "Really? Well, that makes perfect sense."

Chris nodded. "Towards the end, she made me miserable. She tried to have a tight, controlling grip on me and what I did. We got into some pretty bad fights, and she loved to spin the narrative into me being the bad guy when all she did was critique every little thing I did. She didn't start acting like that until after we got married, but the more I thought about it, there were subtle signs of this before we got hitched. So, marriage wasn't the sole reason we didn't work out, even though I always thought it was."

Sarah took a deep breath and hugged Chris. "I'm so glad we had this conversation. Let's get to the parade before we miss everything," she said as she took his hand and hurried down the boardwalk.

They managed to find Margaret, Dave, Harper, Abby, and Donna and Dale, and squeezed in with everyone just as the many basset hounds, the stars of the parade, came down the boardwalk.

Sarah smiled as she saw basset hounds dressed in Hawaiian shirts, some in super hero costumes, then others being pulled in elaborately decorated wagons. She looked over to see Margaret snapping photos of the dogs and Donna pointing them out to Dale. Then, she turned around to see Chris, not looking at the dogs, but looking straight at her, smiling.

CHAPTER TWELVE

Early Easter morning, the beach Easter egg hunt that Liz and Margaret planned was underway. It seemed the whole community knew about it, as there were tons of people with kids in attendance.

Liz and Margaret stood shoulder to shoulder as they looked at all the colorful plastic-filled Easter eggs all over the beach and waited for the eight o'clock start time.

Margaret bit her lip. "Well, there aren't many places to hide eggs on sand, that's for sure."

Liz smiled. "It's perfect for the little ones, and the bigger kids will have fun picking up as many as they can. It's the quintessential beach town egg hunt."

Margaret nodded. "So, Irene and Jackie called out sick. They both have the stomach bug, been throwing up all night."

"You're kidding," Liz said.

Margaret shook her head. "It's been so busy with everything, I just checked my messages from last night a moment ago when we finished hiding all of the eggs."

Liz sighed. "Well, we still have Dolly and Kim. They're busy inside keeping an eye on the brunch dishes in the oven. Where's Bonnie again?"

"She's in Delaware with family," Margaret said as she looked over to see Sarah and Chris walking up with Sam in tow.

"Hey, guys. So glad you came!" Margaret said as she and Liz hugged them.

Sarah smiled and tussled Sam's hair. "Turns out, Sam really wanted to come today. So, we made it happen. He has to go to his mom's afterwards."

"Perfect. Harper and Abby are over there," Margaret said while pointing behind her. Sam took that as his cue to run and join them at the start line.

"And my boys are at home. I guess their Easter egg hunting days are over," Liz said with an exaggerated frown.

Chris chuckled, then looked at Sarah. "There's something over there by the jetty I wanted to show you." He turned to Margaret and Liz. "Do you mind keeping any eye on Sam?"

"Of course," Liz blurted out. "We still have ten minutes before we begin."

Chris led Sarah about a hundred feet away, next to the jetty.

Sarah glanced around. "Well, this is … beachy. What do you want to show me?"

Chris nervously looked at the sky, then at Sarah. "Well, um, I want you to enjoy the peaceful sound of the water against the rocks here."

Sarah shifted her eyes and laughed "Um … OK …."

After what felt like an hour, but was really two minutes, there it was. A plane flying over the ocean pulling a banner behind it.

Sarah looked up to see it. There, for everyone on the beach to see, the banner read *Sarah, will you marry me?*

Sarah held her hand over her mouth as she looked at the plane flying by. "Chris, look at that banner. There's another Sarah getting proposed to," she said cluelessly as Chris kneeled before her.

"I wanted to do this the right way, on my own terms with the ring I specifically picked out just for you."

Sarah threw her head back and laughed with pure happiness before kneeling down next to Chris to hug and kiss him, not even looking at the ring. "I can't believe you did this."

Chris smiled. "I wanted to. Take a look at the ring."

Sarah held the ring box up to her face. It was everything she could ever want out of an engagement ring. It was a classic gold band with a simple solitaire stone. She looked down at the ring that was already on her hand, which was the complete opposite. It was quite a bit more flashy, which apparently was what Donna liked.

"How did you know that this is the kind of engagement ring I've always wanted?" Sarah asked as she slipped on the new ring and put the old one back in the box.

Chris scratched his chin. "You don't remember? When were first met, we ran into some friends of yours at a restaurant. One of them had just become engaged. You looked at her ring, and said it was exactly what you would want. Classic with no frills."

Sarah smiled wide. "You were listening? I thought you were talking to her husband. I remember you two both seeming to be in your own world discussing boats."

Chris nodded, feeling proud of himself. "Oh, I was talking to him, but I was also listening to what you said somehow."

They stood up together, then hugged as cheers came from the crowd that had gathered for the Easter egg hunt.

Chris laughed as he led Sarah back towards everyone. "I guess we had an audience the whole time, huh?"

Just then, it started drizzling, and the sky became overcast. Liz stood in front of everyone and held up her hands. "OK, everyone. We've got to do this before the rain starts. Get ready."

Margaret chimed in. "On your mark. Get set. Go!"

And just like that, the scramble was on with kids all over

the beach trying to get as many of the hundreds of eggs as they could before the sky opened up with a downpour.

* * *

An hour later, the crowd had left, and the rain had started. Margaret and Liz rushed up the porch stairs to the Seahorse to get everything ready for the Easter brunch.

Dolly rushed out of the inn to greet them as they approached the front door. "Guys, we have a serious problem."

Margaret and Liz froze. "What?"

"Something is wrong with our ovens. When the timer went off a few minutes ago, we took everything out, but it was all burnt to a crisp. It's the strangest thing. The oven was set to 375, so I don't know how this could have happened," Dolly said, feeling frustrated.

Margaret held her hand over her mouth. "This happened once at my house. Dave had to recalibrate to fix the issue. He's with his parents at the marina, but I'll call to see if he can get over here. How are we going to get this brunch ready in time, though?"

Liz picked up her phone and called Greg. "I have an idea, but we're going to have to put some appetizers out in the meantime."

Ten minutes later, Greg arrived soaking wet from running through the rain, holding his bag with chef's knives and apron, and Dave was right behind him.

Dave went right to work on the ovens as Greg cleared off the entire kitchen island, then opened the fridge. "Can I use whatever I want out of here?"

Liz and Margaret nodded. "Yes. Pick anything you can throw together for this Easter brunch," Liz said.

Margaret put out the fruit salads and cheese and crackers while Liz, Dolly, and Kim set up a coffee and juice station.

Greg chopped some potatoes and peppers as Dale and Donna walked into the kitchen.

"Hi, guys! Happy Easter! What are you doing here?" Liz asked surprised.

Greg cut in from his loud busy kitchen. "I asked Dale to help me for an hour."

"He did," Dale said as he set down his chef's knives and put on his apron. "We'll have everything ready in a jiffy."

Donna shrugged. "I came along to help out with anything you guys need."

Ten minutes later, Dave popped up from one of the ovens. "I think they're fixed. I remembered how to recalibrate them from all those years ago, surprisingly."

As the B&B guests both at the Seahorse and the Morning Dew Cottage mingled around the appetizers and talked, Dale and Greg feverishly got to work making home fries, French toast, and egg casseroles.

Soon, there was a huge, exquisite Easter brunch buffet set up in the dining room, and Margaret, Liz, Dolly, and Kim breathed a sigh of relief.

* * *

That afternoon, Judy rushed around the house as Bob opened up the oven to check on the ham.

"Bob, it's raining," Judy said as she stopped to look out the front door.

"Yes, I know, hon. It's been raining since this morning," Bob said as he swiped some spinach dip with a piece of pumpernickel bread.

Judy watched as the rain poured down, causing a mini river to form on the side of the streets that raced down to the storm drains. "I don't think I have enough seating for everyone. I lost track of who's coming and who's not."

Bob shrugged. "I could have told you that. I thought we were going to have the whole town over for a minute there."

Judy gave Bob a look. "It's fine. The kids can sit on the couch and eat with the tray tables. That should free up some space. However, now all that seating outside isn't going to work with this rain."

Bob walked to the back door and opened it. "Come here and take a look."

Judy headed over to Bob and peered outside. "We rented this humongous tent and it's set up against the house on the patio. It's even enclosed with some heaters if needed. They'll be perfectly dry."

Judy walked outside under the tent, listening to the rain pitter-patter all over it. "Well, it's kind of dark out here."

Bob thought for a moment. "I have that big bin of patio string lights. I can put them around the perimeter."

Judy nodded and sighed. "OK. That works. I just can't get over the fact that it had to rain the year I'm hosting Easter."

Just then, they heard voices inside. "Judy! Bob!"

Judy ran inside to see Linda, Mike, Mike's parents, Carol, Jack, Debbie, and Phil all hanging up their rain jackets on the rack.

"Well, well, well. So glad you could all make it," Judy said, a smile plastered on her face.

Debbie grinned as she took her two casserole dishes into the kitchen along with Linda and Carol. "We wouldn't miss it for the world."

Carol burst out laughing. "Except Linda. She'd miss it. Then, she wouldn't answer her phone when you called her."

Everyone laughed at that, even Linda. "I'm sorry, everyone. I'll have you know my phone is currently on and will be staying on."

Phil clapped, prompting the rest of the siblings to join in. "Hooray!" they all yelled before going back to laughing again.

Moments later, a gaggle of cousins arrived. Then some

family members from Bob's side, then Liz and Greg and the boys, Margaret and Dave and the girls, Marge and Roger, Betty and Hugh, a few neighbors. It was a packed house through and through.

As the house became completely crowded, Bob looked at all the food piling up on the kitchen counter and set up another table under the tent to put it all on.

After dinner, dessert, and plenty of conversation, Margaret glanced outside to see the rain had stopped and the sun was shining brighter than ever. She stepped outside into the warm sunshine, out of the noisy house with Dave.

"Look at this. It's gorgeous," Margaret said, holding her hands up in the air, trying to feel every bit of the sun's rays.

Dave nodded. "There's even a nice spring breeze. Perfect weather for kite flying."

Margaret's eyes widened. "Let's take the girls to fly kites over by the lighthouse."

Dave smiled. "Great idea, but we'll have to invite my parents. They'll want to go."

"My parents too," Margaret said.

"Well, gee. Let's just extend the invite to everyone. Whoever wants to meet us over there can come. I'll leave now and get the kites from our house," Dave said as he ran inside to get his keys.

"OK, I'll go in and tell everyone," Margaret said as she followed behind him.

Twenty minutes later, everyone from Judy and Bob's house stood on a large grassy area right next to the Cape May Lighthouse on a beautiful spring day.

Dave handed out three kites, and kept one for himself, Margaret, and the girls.

Margaret watched as the others with kites started trying to get them up in the sky.

Meanwhile, Abby and Harper ran with their kite while Dave held on to the end. Finally, it slowly caught the wind and went up. Dave kept giving it more slack until it was high up in the sky, sailing with the other kites.

Harper ran back towards Dave and Margaret. "Can I hold the end?"

"Sure," Dave said as he handed it over and put his arm around Margaret.

Margaret smiled as she looked over at her family. "Look, your parents just got a turn to fly one of the kites."

Dave looked over. "Aw, they're having fun. Is that Betty and Hugh next to them?"

Margaret nodded. "Yep. They talked almost the entire time at dinner. I think they became fast friends."

Dave chuckled. "Look at your parents. Your dad is trying to chase your mom with the kite. I don't think she wants to fly it."

Margaret laughed. "I've never seen my dad with so much energy. All of that walking and jogging is making him much more youthful."

Dave sighed and smiled as he looked at Margaret. "Today couldn't have been any more perfect. Even down to the brunch fiasco and the rain."

Margaret smiled. "You're right about the rain. I enjoyed it. It added character to the day and made this sunshine that much nicer. But then again, you know me. I'm the gardener. I always love rain."

EPILOGUE

It was late April and Margaret was outside watching Dave plow land for their gardens. They'd moved into their new house last summer, so they hadn't had the chance to get the full garden planted. This year would be different, and they were ready.

Dave stopped plowing with the tractor, hopped off, and approached Margaret. "So, this is going to be pretty huge, isn't it?"

Margaret nodded. "Are you up for it? I want to grow even more than we did at Liz and Greg's."

Dave smiled. "Oh, you know I live for this stuff. We can have flower beds, herb beds, tomato beds, whatever you want."

Margaret sighed happily and looked off to the side. "I still want that raised bed kitchen garden right off the house here. Somewhere I can quickly grab what I need when we cook, you know?"

Dave hopped back onto the tractor. "Oh, that's on my list. Already ordered the lumber for it. You sure you want so many beds, though?"

Margaret drifted off into a daydream of hanging freshly laundered sheets to dry on a clothesline, then stopping off at her raised garden bed to admire all her plants. There was something romantic about it. Something that the in-ground garden wasn't, though, both were equally amazing.

"I'm sure. I have so many ideas for this. Do you think it will be done in time?" Margaret asked.

Dave nodded. "Oh yeah. I'm going to start on it when the wood gets delivered in a few days. It's going to be great. By the way, what are we going to do with everything we grow?"

Margaret shrugged. "Well, we'll eat it, put the flowers in vases around the house, give them out to family and friends, and maybe just maybe, we can make a new farm stand. That's down the road, though."

Just then, Margaret's phone rang, and she picked it up while Dave took that as his cue to start up the tractor and drive it to another plot of land to plow.

"Hey, Donna!"

"Hey. What are you up to?" Donna asked as she sat on her couch flipping through a bridal magazine.

"We're getting our gardens ready for the season. It's so exciting to finally get this farm area underway. I can't wait to get my hands in the soil just like we did at Liz and Greg's. Actually, it's gonna be even bigger and better than what we had there," Margaret said.

Donna cleared her throat. "That's wonderful. I can't wait to see it. So, I bit the bullet and told Dale I'm ready to start planning our wedding."

"Oh, that's great. Let me know if I can be of any help. Maybe we can put together flower arrangements from the garden or something."

Donna nodded. "Actually, I was thinking something along those lines, except, how would you feel if we wanted to have our wedding on your land?"

"Really?" Margaret asked, feeling both flattered and shocked. "Our land is where you want to have your wedding?"

Donna sighed. "Dale and I have been discussing this a lot

this past week, and we were both torn between a farm-style rustic wedding and a beach wedding, but ultimately the farm won out ... for now. However, everything is booked."

Margaret thought for a moment. "Booked? When are you planning to get married?"

Donna paused. "Fourth of July. Everyone is usually off from work anyway. I've just always thought that would be a cool day to get married, you know?"

Margaret smiled. "Let me talk to Dave. This could very well work out, but we'll have to discuss logistics first."

* * *

Pick up **Book 13** in the Cape May Series**, Cape May Sunsets,** to follow Margaret, Liz, the rest of the familiar bunch, and some new characters.

ABOUT THE AUTHOR

Claudia Vance is a writer of women's fiction and clean romance. She writes feel good reads that take you to places you'd like to visit with characters you'd want to get to know.

She lives with her boyfriend and two cats in a charming small town in New Jersey, not too far from the beautiful beach town of Cape May. She worked behind the scenes on television shows and film sets for many years, and she's an avid gardener and nature lover.

Printed in the USA
CPSIA information can be obtained
at www.ICGtesting.com
LVHW040744121223
766287LV00043B/1114